AFRICAN WRITERS SERIES LIST

Founding editor · Chinua Achebe

Keys to Signs

Novels are unmarked
*Short Stories
†Poetry
‡Plays
§Autobiography or Biography

AFRICAN WRITERS SERIES

136

The Blinkards

Kobina Sekyi

THE BLINKARDS

Introduction by J. Ayo Langley

LONDON · IBADAN · NAIROBI · LUSAKA

HEINEMANN

Heinemann Educational Books Ltd
48 Charles Street, London WIX 8AH
P.M.B. 5205 Ibadan • P.O. Box 45314 Nairobi.
P.O. Box 3966 Lusaka

EDINBURGH MELBOURNE AUCKLAND TORONTO
HONG KONG SINGAPORE KUALA LUMPUR
NEW DELHI

ISBN 0 435 90136 2

First published by Rex Collings Ltd 1974
First published in African Writers Series 1974

Printed in Belgium
by Les Presses St Augustin,
Bruges DF 6894

FOREWORD

In an essay about himself William Hazlitt once began 'It is a hard and a nice thing to write of one's self'. I find it not much less so to write of one's father — especially where one is, as I am, completely lost in filial and, as I often fear, uncritical admiration. With me every memory of him is not only cherished, but remains as vivid, twenty years after I last saw him, as when I used to question him about things like the Social Contract, in my undergraduate days, and listened, with some incomprehension to his, as I thought then, rather odd views. I often dream about him — but never remember till I wake up that he died many years ago. It is all so real.

Therefore I have rarely dared to write anything seriously on this subject, despite its perennial fascination for me, because I am always haunted by the horror of failing to summon the requisite objectivity. But Dr Ayo Langley has all that, and a great deal more besides, as I have found — objectivity, painstaking and thoroughgoing scholarship, a keen, critical faculty, together, despite all that, with an admiration for the subject only less unbounded than my own. I am delighted as well as thankful that he has chosen and offered to edit the play, whose publication is largely due to his initiative.

The Blinkards is a satire — It satirizes, thoughtfully but mercilessly, a kind of social epidemic which first appeared along with the missionaries in the lives of our forbears in the eighteen fifties, gathered strength through the rest of the nineteenth century, and raged in the opening decades of the twentieth. It began with the total rejection of African religious belief in favour of Christianity; it went on to the total confusion of Christianity with Christendom — of all that was good with all that was European; and the sequel, in our generation has been to extend, or tend to extend, this confusion from the social sphere to the political, and to accept no political ideologies not borrowed from the one or the other of the two parts into which Christendom finally divided, the Eastern or the Western side of the Iron Curtain.

The rebellion against this trend set in not long after it began and ironically enough it first became articulate in the same part of the country which was first affected. Among its exponents were James Hutton Brew, John Mensah Sarbah, Attoh-Ahuma, Casely Hayford, and his disciple, Kobina Sekyi (Egya, as he was always known to his children and some close friends, and as I should now call him). By 1915 already the philosopher and sociologist he never ceased at heart to be, Egya insisted that society was an organism, living, growing, developing, evolving. It evolved healthily only if it reacted correctly to the stimuli from its changing environment. But in that process it never abruptly replaces whole limbs with borrowed ones, still less annihilate its whole self, but evolves in its various parts, without ever doing damage or violence to its organic structure, the right adaptations to its changing context — particularly the great changes caused by the 'juxtaposition of the two civilizations', as he put it somewhere in his writings. Merely to substitute the tail of a lizard for that of a fish is a false reaction — not a natural adaptation to any change in the environment but an absurd and monstrous innovation, resulting not in some healthier new creature, but in a mere abortion, unlikely to survive in the struggle for existence. In Egya's view it is the same with society and manners; and he saw our conscious and thoroughgoing imitation of European manners and European society as the social analogue of that physical monstrosity.

Of course Egya went much further. He applied the full rigours of this line of thought to the political, no less than the social aspect of the social organism. He concluded early, and stuck to that conclusion with a tenacity few understood and many found irritating, that it was the traditional political institutions themselves, and not anything adventitious, which being the valid results of our society's long evolution in its environment should, by further natural evolution, by unconstricted adaptation to the changing environment and the new stimuli, form the basis of the future polity, whatever form that may finally take. And this brings me to one of the few points on which I would venture to disagree with the accomplished editor. For Dr. Langley expresses the view that Egya was unable 'to emerge as a national leader (assuming he wanted to)' because he was 'trapped in Cape Coast by the ideology and organization of an institution that had long outlived its usefulness' — meaning by that the 'moribund' Aborigines Rights Protection Society of which Egya eventually became the last President but one.

I believe, and what Dr Langley writes elsewhere suggests he might agree with this, that Egya's non-emergence in the practical politics of the later days was owing, not to some more archaic brand of practical politics, as seems suggested, but to those deeply held convictions of his own political and social philosophy. That is where I would put the emphasis. For all his dogged opposition to indirect rule in all its forms, Egya was always more the political thinker engrossed with the search for the correct than the practical politician, preoccupied with the art of the possible. The rewards of practical politics seemed to matter less to him than the awakening of his countrymen to the importance of correct political, no less than correct social evolution. If indirect rule threatened our correct political evolution by the perversion of Chieftaincy, like a virus attacking the evolving organism in a most vital part, then the correct strategy was to rid the organism of the virus, and by this cure allow the damaged tissues to resume their normal and healthy growth, and the entire organism its normal and healthy evolution. To him the correct answer was certainly not to excise the vital organs in the hope of successfully transplanting those of a different organism — for that would be to perpetrate, in the political life of our society, the analogue of that monstrosity in its social life, that social abortion, lampooned in *The Blinkards*.

This view of our African society as an organism whose survival and salvation lies essentially in adapting to its modern world-context by correct (and untrammelled) evolution, this evolutionist ideal, I believe is the key to the enigma which the author's seemingly complex and certainly many sided personality presented to many. Except in the cool month of August, or in the higher courts of law where wigs and gowns were de rigueur, he wore his native togas at all times, whether attending a meeting of the Paramount Chiefs council (of which he was a member) whether appearing before the lower courts (where his garb is said to have irritated some magistrates) or relaxing at home to the music of Coleridge-Taylor or Richard Wagner on old seventy-eights. At once a lover of our traditional cuisine and a connoisseur of good cigars and good wine, he spoke the vernacular whenever he did not have to speak English. He vastly admired the more outstanding illiterate chiefs of the older school for a certain statesmanlike sagacity. But he also admired the Greek philosophers, immensely enjoyed Anatole France, and I always found him an ardent collector of good European literature for which he had an avid and omnivorous appetite. Some observers find him an élitist; others a populist. The European man-on-the-spot called him 'a Cape Coast lawyer, able intelligent and well educated, but with a most pronounced anti-European complex. The European intellectual called him 'the outstanding example of a tragic and unresolved conflict desiring at once to be pagan and Christian, aboriginal and European, Akan Traditionalist and Western progressive'. I think he was neither tragic, nor unresolved, nor a conflict, any more than modern Japan or the modern Japanese is tragic or unresolved or a conflict. I believe he was just an instance of the kind adaptive evolution by which new civilizations quickly burst into flower and old ones are preserved from decay and extinction, and which he himself believed to be the right answer. I believe he was Mr Onyimdzi, the young lawyer in *The Blinkards*; and, to find out what is really meant by that, I hope you will turn now to the introduction and then to the play.

H.V.H. SEKYI
ST JOHN'S WOOD, LONDON
December 1973

> *"O, wad some pow'r the giftie gi'e us*
> *Tae see oursel as ithers see us"*
>
> BURNS

PERSONS REPRESENTED

MR BROFUSEM	A Merchant
MR ONYIMDZI	A Young Barrister
MR TSIBA	A Cocoa Magnate
DR ONWEYIE	A Physician and Surgeon
MR OKADU	A Young Blood
NYAMIKYE	Servant to Mr Brofusem
HALF-CROWN	A Krooboy, servant to Mr Onyimdzi
MRS BROFUSEM	A Leader of Fashion
MISS TSIBA	Daughter to Mr Tsiba
NNA SUMPA	Wife to Mr Tsiba and mother to Miss Tsiba
NANA KATAWIRWA	Mother to Ena Sumpa

A Parson
Officers and Members of the 'Cosmopolitan Club'
Some *Ahyentariu*, old and Young, Male and Female
Some Female *Atamfurafu*
An Old Fisherman
Two Young Fishermen
Some boys
A Policeman
A White Man

Place: CAPE COAST
Time: THE PRESENT

INTRODUCTION

The smart professionals in three piece,
Sweating away their humanity in driblets,
And wiping the blood from their brow
  We have found a new land
  This side of eternity
  And our songs are dying on our lips.
Standing at hellgate you watch those who seek admission
Still the familiar faces that watched and gave you up
As one who had let the side down
'Come on, old boy, you cannot dress like that.'
And tears well in my eyes for them
These who want to be seen in the best company
Have adjured the magic of being themselves
And in the new land we have found
The water is drying from the towel
Our songs are dead and we sell them dead to the other side
Reaching for the Stars we stop at the house of Moon
And pause to relearn the wisdom of our fathers.

George Awoonor-William's poem 'We have found a new land' can be said to constitute the 'message', as well as a statement of the main ideas and dilemmas Kobina Sekyi sought to dramatize in his 1915 satirical play *The Blinkards*. William Esuman-Gwira Sekyi, better known as Kobina Sekyi, is one African writer and controversialist who has never appeared in anthologies of African literature (except in Nancy Cunard's 1934 anthology, *Negro*) and in recent commentaries on African literature. A further index of Sekyi's obscurity, and of our ignorance of the few pre-1930 African literary intellectuals, is his non-appearance in Janheinz Jahn's *A bibliography of Neo-African literature* and *A History of Neo-African literature*. Although he rarely appears in histories of nationalism in West Africa,

Sekyi was one of the most outstanding and most controversial members of the West African nationalist intelligentsia between 1920 and 1952. It is therefore in the context of this many-sided intelligentsia of lawyers, literati, doctors, journalists and clergymen that his writings and activities should be studied and assessed.

William Esuman-Gwira Sekyi, grandson on his father's side of Chief Kofi Sekyi, was born on 1 November 1892 at Cape Coast, cradle of Gold Coast nationalism. His mother, Wilhelmina Pietersen, was the daughter of a wealthy Gold Coast merchant, W.E. Pietersen of Pietersen and Co. The surname, Sekyi (the anglicized form of which was Sackey) originated from his paternal grandfather's name, the proper spelling of which he adopted with the latter's permission. Sekyi was also a nephew of Henry Van Hein, a successful businessman, as well as a leading member of the Cape Coast nationalist school. Up to 1909-1910, Sekyi attended Mfantsipim boys' school, founded in 1876 as a boarding school and named Wesleyan High School, under the principalship of James Picot. One of the earliest pupils was John Mensah Sarbah, one of Ghana's early patriots and the first African exponent of customary law. As the school was closed for financial reasons in 1884 and only reopened in 1893 (now renamed Cape Coast Collegiate School) we can assume that young Sekyi attended it between 1903 and 1909, and matriculated before he was twenty for the University of London.[1] Sekyi himself states in the preface to his unpublished *The Meaning of the Expression 'Thinking in English'* (1937) that the other boys were bigger and older and

1. The school was closed in 1903 and only re-opened in 1905 through the efforts of J. Mensah Sarbah and his Fante Public Schools Trust. The founders hoped that the school would follow 'closely the model of the great Public Schools of England', though it was hoped that technical and commercial education would be emphasized as well.

[2]

that he himself was rather studious. Other accounts[2] portray young Sekyi as a precocious, extremely bright boy, always selected as the natural leader by the others. From his poems, particularly the one entitled 'The Sojourner' (1918) and his short story, *The Anglo-Fanti* serialized in *West Africa* in 1918 by his friend Cartwright, the editor, and in Nancy Cunard's anthology, *Negro*, in 1934, we know that he was brought up as an Anglo-African in a society whose educated members were brought up to believe that all things African were retrograde and were to be despised, and that thorough anglicization (and Christianization) was the passport to 'civilization' and 'progress'. The evidence available so far indicates that Sekyi accepted these values and, I am informed, even turned up for a school photograph in good old Edwardian collar and woollen suit, much to the chagrin of the Reverend W. Turnbull Balmer, who had always taught his small class of eight boys, called 'The Faithful Eight' (because they went to school regularly and taught each other when the school closed for lack of funds and teachers) to cherish their indigenous customs, history, languages and modes of dress. Up to 1910, therefore, when Sekyi sailed for England to study he was, as he later confessed in 'The Sojourner' and subsequent socio-political writings, an 'Anglomaniac' who had been brought up and indoctrinated to be ashamed of most things African.

It is interesting to note that Sekyi's choice of subject for his first degree at University College, London, was English literature. This was in 1910-11. Shortly after taking up the subject, however, he was persuaded by a fellow African student, Delo Dosumu, from Nigeria, to give it up and take up philosophy. Dosumu, son of a prosperous Lagos merchant had entered the university a year before Sekyi and was reading

2. Interview with W. S. Kwesi Johnson, Cape Coast, September 1969.

for an honours degree in philosophy. He became the first African to graduate in philosophy in a British university. Sekyi developed a deep passion for philosophy and successfully completed the course in 1913 with a second class honours degree. I was reliably informed by the late C.H. Hayfron-Benjamin, a close friend of Sekyi and a former editor of *The Gold Coast Observer*, that Sekyi was well thought of by Professor Dawes-Hicks, then head of the philosophy department. Copies of some of Sekyi's speeches and articles, as well as some remarks in his poems indicate that Sekyi underwent an identity crisis and ideological transformation (or reconversion) within a short time of his arrival in London. Britain swiftly disillusions him, even he tells us, 'his old dreams as to European food are over'; landladies worry him no end, and the regular baths he has been accustomed to become a problem, as the 'wash' is hardly a satisfactory substitute. But, more devastatingly, 'it does not take him long to find out he is regarded as a savage even by the starving unemployed who ask him for alms', and many are the stupid questions he is asked about his humanity;[3] 'on the whole he is much disappointed with England as he has seen it by the time he is six months in England' — just about the normal period it takes the observant and thinking black student to reach the same conclusion. Sekyi discussed his disillusionment and the implications of his increasing sense of identity with his fellow African students; a few understood and tried to analyse the alien society in relation to Sekyi's basic question 'Who am I?', but the majority of his fellow-students, alas, as usual, mistook the shadow and fringes for

3. Kobina Sekyi: "Extracts from 'The Anglo-Fanti' (a psychological study of a type of present-day Gold Coastian who has been educated partly in the English manner)" in Nancy Cunard: *Negro* (Wishart and Co., London, 1934) p. 775; published in full in *West Africa*, May-July 1918.

the core and substance of what they thought to be English culture. Sekyi leaves us in no doubt that he disapproved of their trendy pointed shows, frequenting of dance halls and general involvement with proletarian culture. Naturally as a proud African from a well-to-do and westernized Cape Coast family he would not fraternize with the working class, not even with H.M.'s imperial working class. As sociology was one of his subjects, it is perhaps not surprising that Sekyi showed a keen interest in the intricacies of British society and culture. He certainly knew the difference between aristocrats, middle classes and imperialistic proletarians. Small wonder his friends nicknamed him 'the George Bernard Shaw of West Africa'. The observant black student, says Sekyi, 'soon begins to distinguish the various distinct grades of society in England...it does not take him long to observe that teaching in Sunday schools in the slums of London lays one open to all sorts of unwelcome attention, amounting to patronage, by civilized people very low on the social scale. He finds out, for example, that religious enthusiam is a form of low class emotion in England... The cockney accent gets on his nerves, and he flies from class meetings where he receives religious ministration in concert with housemaids and domestics.' White women cease to appeal to him because they humiliate him by making him feel they are doing him a favour; as for the church, he is finally driven away from it by 'the unforgettably plebeian stamp of some of his religious associates'. [4] A copy of a speech he made in 1910 in London, entitled 'A Talk to Gold Coast Natives' [5], and 'Morality and Nature', a paper he read in 1913 to the Philosophical Society of King's College, London, and subsequently published in 1914 in *The African Telegraph and*

4. Sekyi, "Extracts from 'The Anglo-Fanti...", op. cit., p. 776.
5. Text kindly supplied by one of Sekyi's sons, His Excellency, H. Van Hein Sekyi.

Gold Coast Mirror edited by Eldred Taylor in London, also indicates Sekyi's changing political and philosophical outlook, and may be said to mark the first stage of his Africanisation of Western philosophy. As Professor K.A.B. Jones-Quartey has argued in an interesting pioneering study of Sekyi, the more European philosophy Kobina Sekyi read, the more African he became. 6

Sekyi's ideological and cultural conflicts, however, were not entirely resolved. Professionally, he was rather ambiguous about his career; on the one hand, as he later admitted, his ambition was to become an engineer, like his mother's younger brother, J. B. Esuman-Gwira; on the other hand, the career expectation of his parents and relatives was different. They had chosen a legal career for him, and as they controlled the purse, the young man had no choice but to give in. 7 In January 1914 his maternal grandfather, W. E. Pietersen, died, leaving him much of the family business and H. Van Hein administered the property, as well as paid for Sekyi's studies and maintenance. Nevertheless Sekyi put up a good fight before returning to Cape Coast in 1913, at the completion of his first degree course. He taught for two years in Cape Coast, wrote articles on social and literary matters, and deliberately reintegrated himself into Akan-Fanti culture. It was towards the end of this interlude that he wrote the play published for the first time in this volume, "*The Blinkards*". In the words of his

6. K.A.B. Jones-Quartey, "Kobina Sekyi: A Fragment of Biography", *Research Review* (University of Ghana), Michaelmas Term, Vol. 4, No. 1, pp. 74-78. For a more systematic exposition of Sekyi's social and political philosophy see J. Ayo Langley, "Modernization and its Malcontents: Kobina Sekyi of Ghana and the Restatement of African Political Theory", paper for Centre of African Studies (University of Edinburgh) Seminar, February 1970, published in *Research Review*, Trinity Term, Vol. 6, 1970.

7. Sekyi to A. F. E. Fieldgate, Commissioner, Central Province, Cape Coast, 8 September 1939. Sekyi Papers, Acc. No. 332/64.

poem "The Sojourner", he was 'Home Again Restored to
Mental Health'. His three years in England were merely a
'lucid interval'. By 1915 the question of his legal career was
settled and he returned to England in late 1915 on the
"S. S. Falaba" in company with some fellow students. It was
while the ship was in the Irish Sea that it was torpedoed by a
German U-Boat; some lives were lost, but Sekyi managed to
clamber on to a life boat. According to interviews with some
of his surviving friends in Cape Coast, it was this incident that
finally convinced Sekyi that African values and interests were
incompatible with those of Europe. I was informed by those to
whom he wrote after the incident that after he had just managed
to get into a lifeboat one of the Europeans started shouting at
him to get off, as he (Sekyi) a black man, had no right to be alive
when whites were drowning. In the view of some of those I
interviewed, this was the traumatic experience that finally led
Sekyi (to use the title of one of his unpublished manuscripts)
to 'the parting of the ways'. His next three years in Britain,
therefore, were as far as he was concerned merely 'the lucid
interval sustained'—to borrow the sub-title of section three of
"The Sojourner".

By mid-1918 Sekyi had qualified as a barrister and had
achieved the distinction of graduating M. A. in philosophy from
his old university, his ethics dissertation being on "The State
and the Individual Considered in the Light of its Bearing on the
Conception of Duty" where he promptly set to question the
European idea of 'progress', law and state as the highest development of society. At the risk of oversimplification, we may
say that Sekyi's argument against this school of thought (and
they included eminent sociologists like L. T. Hobhouse) was
that following Darwin-inspired unilinear theories of social
development, they confused civilization with 'progress', and
the latter with culture, and that what they exalted as hallmarks

of civilization were merely refinements of the superficial and the artificial. The development of statute law and the rise of the modern state and bureaucracy, he argued, had nothing to do with morality and progress but were merely the manifestations of increasing artificiality and decadence.[8] It is significant that these problems of socio-cultural crisis had been occupying the attention of European intellectuals from the 1890s; the post-war years merely witnessed an intensification of the debate.

Within one year of his arrival at Cape Coast the young lawyer was already in nationalist politics and had quickly established himself as an able journalist and controversialist. In long, ponderous sentences (the result of both his philosophical and legal training, as well as his complex personality) he ridiculed, criticised, lampooned and preached. His sharp tongue and vitriolic pen were specially reserved for 'the man on the spot', that exasperatingly pretentious breed of colonial bureaucrats, and the black Englishmen, particularly those he labelled 'rabid Christians'. In 1919-1920 he helped in the launching and organisation of the Gold Coast section of the pan-West African National Congress of British West Africa, and read a paper at the inaugural meeting of the Congress at Accra in March 1920 on "Education with Particular Reference to a West African University". He distinguished himself at that congress, and did much propaganda work on its behalf in the Gold Coast papers in the early 1920s, so much so that J. E. Casely-Hayford, founder of the movement, expressed his 'high appreciation of the great and noble work' Sekyi had done on behalf of Congress, concluding that 'it is a matter of

8. See *The State and the Individual...* (University of London, 1918, unpublished thesis); "Morality and Nature", *The African Telegraph and Gold Coast Mirror* (London) December 1914, p. 26 and January 1915; also "The Future of Subject Peoples", *The African Times and Orient Review* (London) October-December, 1917. In general see J. Ayo Langley, "Modernization and its Malcontents...", op. cit.

great encouragement to me that there are high-souled men of this generation who are prepared to work for the uplift of this country without regard to any personal gain whatever.'[9] Several patriotic Africans, some unknown to him, wrote to him for advice, or sought his co-operation in various educational, literary or social schemes 'towards stimulating the national Consciousness which,' said one of them, 'hitherto has been partially, if not in whole, dormant'.[10] In January 1921 Sekyi submitted his celebrated "Our White Friends" articles which were serialised in the *Gold Coast Leader*, and was in popular demand 'to address the educated community in town' whenever he went. Kojo Thompson and some of the chiefs and older nationalists increasingly came to regard young Sekyi as general spokesman and leading government critic. Professionally, too, the young man was not doing too badly.

Most of Sekyi's ideas, however, ran counter to the prevailing social prejudices. He rejected Christianity (and Islam) when the vast majority uncritically accepted Christianity and all its implications; he desperately wanted a return to the rationality and dignity of the old order, of the ancestors, when the majority of his contemporaries (educated and semi-educated alike) were rushing headlong towards anglicization and 'progress'; he wanted the chiefs who were becoming more autocratic under British rule to return to the more democratic and constitutional practices of the old days, but most of the chiefs, having tasted the heady wine of their colonial masters, were no longer interested in being responsible to the people. And so on. The list of contradictions in the colonial society of the time (and

9. J. E. Casely-Hayford to Kobina Sekyi, 26 March 1921, Sekyi Papers, Cape Coast, Acc. No. 571/64.
10. Karew Acquaah to Sekyi, 14 January 1921, ibid.

today) is endless, and Sekyi's vast journalistic output, and over twelve unpublished manuscripts on law, politics and language clearly illustrate his deep preoccupation with this cultural crisis. Even his literary output (which is very small compared to his political writings) show this preoccupation with politics and culture. This is particularly true of most of the poems he wrote between 1918 and 1952, and of the 1915 light comedy, significantly entitled *The Blinkards*. This remembrance of things past, and the strenuous and consistent attempt to rediscover a lost identity was, paradoxically, both Sekyi's strength and, some would say, his weakness. It was his strength to the extent that he was one of the very few who had the courage and integrity, in the face of so many temptations, to state their principles and seek to live by them, whatever the consequences. He was misunderstood, sometimes maligned, and in his later years, often ignored by the opportunists who had come to terms with the new order, and by the ignorant who thought they knew all the answers. Preoccupation with the past was Sekyi's weakness in that he easily conveyed the impression (particularly among Europeans) of being a fanatic or unprogressive obscurantist. Indeed one English professor who wrote a book on the Gold Coast legislative council in 1948 has labelled him a 'Gandhi manqué'. Of course Sekyi was neither a fanatic nor an unprogressive nationalist; as I have shown elsewhere he believed in modernization, but modernization tempered and controlled by the creative and integrative elements of tradition. Edmund Burke would have been in full agreement with much of Sekyi's political thought. Sekyi 'failed' as a charismatic leader; he 'failed' to lead because he did not want to lead, as he constantly made plain to both Nkrumah and Danquah. He was by nature a philosopher and a guide; politics, as the men who led Ghana to independence saw it, was anathema to him. Right up to the eve of independence, he still clung to his somewhat élitist and patrician view that the natural rulers and the intelligentsia should rule within a federal Ghana, with the executive of the moribund Gold Coast Aborigines Rights Protection Society serving as a cabinet. This, in my view, is the clue to Sekyi's inability to emerge as a national leader (assuming he wanted to). He was trapped in Cape Coast by the ideology and organization of an institution that had long outlived its usefulness. Nevertheless, both the man and his message are of great significance not only for contemporary Ghana but for Africa as a whole. Indeed there was no date on the original copy of *The Blinkards*; it simply read "Place: Cape Coast. Time: The Present". Sekyi died on June 2, 1956.

The Blinkards itself is a light comedy of the Shavian type, it is written in both English and Fante and was staged by members of the Cosmopolitan Club in Cape Coast in 1915. I have so far been unable to trace any contemporary reviews of the play or of the performance; however, as its central ideas on the dangers of Europeanism reflect some of the key ideas of the Cape Coast nationalists who also dominated the press and the literary clubs, one may conclude that the play was well received, particularly as it would have been spiced with telling Fante aphorisms. It is also reasonable to assume that Sekyi provided alternative translations in Fante (and the play may well have been performed entirely in Fante) because of his concern about anglicisation and the inability of the younger generation who had grown up in colonial boarding schools and under missionary influence, to speak the Fante of the ancestors. Moreover, as Sekyi later argued (1937) in "The Meaning of the Expression 'Thinking in English'", language and communication can only be intelligible within a specific socio-cultural context. As Sekyi tries to illustrate in the play through the semi-educated Mrs Brofusem, who like many a

[11]

'been-to' mistakes English working class culture for what she thinks is *the* English culture, and through the overcredulous cocoa farmer Tsiba who is easily taken in by Mrs Brofusem's ludicrous imitation English mannerisms, incomplete understanding of language may lead to all sorts of misunderstandings, distortions and cultural confusion, not to mention false values and irritating social pretentions. As Alexander Pope once put it 'A little learning is a dangerous thing, Drink deep or taste not the Pierian spring. There shallow draughts intoxicate the brain...' This was the class of Anglo-Africans Sekyi regarded with a mixture of pity and contempt, and whom he continuously exhorted, pilloried and despaired of. Here is one example of his sketch of the anglomaniac, taken from "The Sojourner":

A product of the low school embroidered by the high,
Upbrought and trained by similar products, here am I.

I go to school on weekdays (excepting Saturdays),...
I speak English to soften my harsher native tongue,
It matters not if often I speak the Fanti wrong.

I'm learning to be British, and treat with due contempt,
The worship of the Fetish, from which I am exempt.

I was baptised an infant, a Christian hedged around
With prayer from the moment my being was unbound.

I'm clad in coat and trousers, with boots upon my feet;
And *tamfurafu* and Hausas I seldom deign to greet.

For I despise the native that wears the native dress
The badge that marks the bushman, who never will
[progress.

All native ways are silly, repulsive, unrefined,
All customs superstitious, that rule the savage mind.

I like civilization; and I'd be glad to see
All peoples that are pagan eschew idolatry.

[12]

I reckon high the power of Governors and such;
But our own Kings and Chiefs—why they do not matter
[much!
And so you see how loyal a Britisher I've grown…
I soon shall go to England…
And there I'll try my hardest to learn the English life,
And I will try to marry a real English wife!

Thus spoke the anglomaniac, the typical West Coast African so often the object of ridicule in European travellers' accounts of life in colonial British West African society. Sekyi and a few like-minded contemporaries in West Africa[11] constantly returned to this theme of the alienated African in their attempts to warn against the dangers of excessive Europeanization. One particular evil he and his contemporaries always dwelt upon was what they considered to be the demoralizing effect of christianity on African womanhood, and on morals in general. Sekyi was particularly vehement in his condemnation of the 1884 Marriage Ordinance which, he claimed, was inspired by bigoted missionaries, and responsible for the disintegration of the family, individualism and immorality. His views on the matter are more forcefully stated in his *A Comparison of Gold Coast, English and Akan-Fanti Laws in Relation to the Absolute Rights of the Individual* (1937) and *The Meaning of the Expression 'Thinking in English'* (1937). In the former manuscript he endeavoured to show, among other things, that contrary to the European view that African women were little better than chattels, African women, at least in Akan-Fanti custom, had

11. See, for example H. Kwesi Oku, "The kind of Christianity we have in Akan and Akwapim Districts on the Gold Coast", and Ladipo Odunsi, "Britain and the Africans", in Nancy Cunard (ed) *Negro*, op. cit., pp. 772-773 and 769-771. Earlier nationalists like Blyden, Casely-Hayford, S.R.B. Attoh Ahuma, Bishop James Johnson, Mojola Agbebi, Orishatuke Faduma, to name only a few, had expressed similar views.

their rights protected, their roles defined, and indeed exercised important political functions at a time when women were not allowed to vote in Europe.[12] In the latter work he restated, via a mixture of a theory of sociolinguistics and nationalist propaganda, his criticism of some of the follies and problems of European-style marriages contracted by anglicized or semi-anglicized Africans, which is the basic theme of *The Blinkards*. In the words of a Nigerian contemporary 'it was greatly debatable whether the new state and conception of marriage tended to produce a more moral outlook or even happier condition. Everywhere hypocrisy prevailed; since society was being reorganized on its (i.e. missionary) basis, then it must be embraced at all costs, morals must fly to the four winds and a superficial form of European ethics substituted—in these communities, the half-educated were the worst victims. Having learned no trade they were unable to use their hands; they were unfitted for the enviable posts of clerkship and too proud to work with their hands. Attempting to emulate Europeans, they perceived only the external things and wasted their money on woollen suits in a hot climate, carrying their idiosyncrasies in dress far enough to give them the aspects of comic opera characters...'[13] West African coast society, according to Odunsi, exhibited 'all the marks of a decadent pseudo-western civilization'.[14]

12. Incidentally, Sekyi has left us an interesting account of his observation of the suffragette movement while he was a student in England.
13. Lapido Odunsi in Nancy Cunard, *Negro*, op. cit., p. 773.
14. Cf. Sekyi's 1920 Congress paper, "Education with Particular Reference to a West African University", pp. 10-21 in which he complained about the 'new type of African which understands neither what European teaching has left it as a heritage of subservience nor what ancestral Africans had bequeathed as the legitimate inheritance of sons of the soil... [and] how our young men are... dissolute and incline more to the lighter side of European life...', how colonial educational policies were formulated without reference to African

The Blinkards is in three acts, and can be described as 'the made play' of the conventional theatre, the sort of theatre which, supplemented by the concert-type theatre, was popular in West Africa in the 1920s and 40s, and still provides much entertainment today, although new forms of theatre have emerged in Africa in the last ten years. Playwrights and theatrical groups are now experimenting with traditional African forms such as folklore, storytelling, drumming and dancing etc. In the 1920s, however, the intelligentsia hardly thought in these terms. There were indeed some plays and concerts and short stories in Krio in Freetown[15] and in *The Blinkards* the telling Fante proverbs and allusions do much to enrich and enliven the play, as well as drive home the author's moral point of view; and one may well imagine a Cape Coast audience in 1915 rolling with laughter or even contributing some home-spun philosophy in the usual African dialogue between actors (or storyteller) and audience.[16] As Sekyi was not only a cultural nationalist but was genuinely interested in good literature and creative writing, one may assume that his aim was not only to entertain but to instruct and provoke debate on major socio-cultural problems.

After re-reading the play, and on further discussion with more competent authorities, I have decided to leave the original play substantially as it stands. As I am not a Fanti speaker, I have taken advice from Ghanaian authorities as to the moder-

institutions and ideas, and how that education had produced 'frock ladies', that class of African women he compared to the 'hideous and unsexed abortions which the so-called higher education of women in Europe has produced'.

15. See Eldred Jones, "Freetown—the Contemporary Cultural Scene" in C. Fyfe and Eldred Jones (eds.), *Freetown: A Symposium* (Sierra Leone University Press, Freetown, 1968), p. 206.

16. For the social function of Comic Plays in Ghana see K. N. Bame, "The Popular Theatre in Ghana", *Research Review* (University of Ghana), Lent Term, Vol. 3, No. 2, 1967, 34-38.

nization of Sekyi's Fanti orthography in those sections of the play where the Fanti translations have been retained for the Ghana edition. Needless to say, this has been handled as judiciously as possible to prevent loss of dramatic effect, and of meaning. Secondly, with regard to characterization, the modern reader may object that some of the characters have been portrayed either as too naive e.g. Tsiba the cocoa farmer (who one would assume was an unlikely Cape Coast cocoa farmer, or possibly an absentee one), or, like Mrs Brofusem, are too grotesque. One must, however, make some allowance here, bearing in mind the social composition and intellectual outlook of Sekyi's audience and his perception of his role in that particular society, as well as his general aim of satirizing slowly and painfully, the type of African woman British colonial education and missionary activity had produced. In the case of Tsiba, perhaps one can criticise Sekyi for over-doing the caricature. Sekyi was very much prejudiced against the new class of businessmen and cocoa merchants produced by the colonial economy. In his view, imperial commerce and christianity were the two principal agents of social disintegration in West Africa. [17] Indeed one of his unpublished plays is entitled *Blacks and Commerce*. Another volume of short stories he wrote between 1920 and 1930, entitled *Sketches of West African Life* should have been published by George Allen and Unwin, but it seems publishing costs were too high, particularly during the depression. Unfortunately, I have been unable to trace this volume. The nearest I have come to locating it is a four page manuscript at Cape Coast with the title *Sketches of Life in West Africa* subtitled "The Peace of Our Lord the King" in which, as in *The Blinkards*, the debate is on the

17. See Sekyi's 'The Future of Subject Peoples", *The African Times and Orient Review* (London) October-December 1917, and "Education in British West Africa", ibid., July 1917, pp. 33-35.

theme of tradition and modernity and is a story about two brothers; the elder borther is brought up in the traditional way and the younger under a catechist and 'had grown to regard his brother as backward'. The younger brother became a clerk in a trading establishment and had 'eventually made many unsuccessful ventures at independent trading during the days of the "booms" which at intervals occurred in those regions. He had exercised his full rights as a semi-educated African and had weakened his body considerably in consequence'. Sekyi deals with the fortunes of the brothers as they play their roles within the traditional socio-political system. Needless to say, the elder brother proved to be the better man, morally and materially. The Mrs Brofusem of *The Blinkards* was also one of the characters of another story, three or four pages of which I was able to read. That story bears the title *Nicodemus Anastatius Hilson: A Tale of West Africa*.[18]

Taking into consideration our analysis of Sekyi's social and political thought, then, we may describe *The Blinkards* as an attempt to popularize and dramatize his criticism of the social and cultural consequences of colonialism, and his view of the relationship between freedom, culture and morality. Small wonder, that with Robert Burns, whom he quotes with approval in the play, Sekyi prayed that

'...some pow'r the giftie gi'e us
Tae see oursel as ithers see us.'

J. Ayo Langley   Edinburgh June, 1971

---

18. See Sekyi Papers, Acc. No. 618/64 and 556/64, Ghana National Archives, Cape Coast. Eight pages of another story, *The Stolen Familiar* Archives, Cape Coast. Eight pages of another story, *The Stolen Familiar—A Tale of Witchcraft in West Africa*, can be found in Acc. No. 520/64

ENGLISH
TRANSLATION

NYAM (...) I wonder why I always find cigar-ashes here, when
I come to dust this room always. I shall sweep them up once
more and see if there will be any more tomorrow. I should
like to know what is the use of sweeping a room which is
never clean. (...) What a pretty book this is! (...) I'll open
it. (...) O! What are these dried leaves in the book for?
I suppose they are to be swept away—I'll pick them up.

MRS BROF Look here, you idiot, what are you up to? Give me
those leaves (...) You are too much of a bushman. Havn't I
told you that, in England, leaves are placed in books to dry,
the books when the leaves are dry, being placed in the
drawing rooms? (...) And what have you swept up those
ashes for? How often do you want me to tell you that cigar-
ashes are good for carpets? Do you not know that, in England,
cigar-ashes are used to kill the moths in the carpets? (...)
You are a great nuisance. Get out of this room (...) How
sweet this room looks (...) When I reflect that our fore-
fathers had only *ntwima* to scour their floors with, and had

[18]

[ACT ONE]

SCENE ONE
Mrs Brofusem's Drawing-room. Doors R & L.

Enter Nyamikye, in short knickers and singlet, with dust-pan and brush. L.

NYAM *(Sweeping)* Ndaansa 'i mibesiesie ha/ara/a, nna m'ehu sigyar nsu de ogugu ha. Abenadzi ntsir e? Miripra bio su'ahwe se ekyina su mibeba abotu 'bi su a? Waansee su na nyimpa bepra mbre eho ntsiw da. *(Sees a nicely-bound book)* A! Buukuw 'i ye few ai! *(Places brush and pan on floor, and takes up book).* Murubwei m' m'ahwe *(Opens book. Some dried leaves fall out)* O! Ahaban kyinkyinii 'i a ogu m'i su e? Gyema iwura a. Kyire M'intasi *(Replaces book, and picks up dried leaves).*

Enter Mrs Brofusem, in a loose European undress gown, lorgnette on nose. L.

MRS BROF Nhwe, iguan o, eriye den? Fa ahaban n'ma m'. *(Takes leaves from Nyamikye).* Ewu eye disinyi dudu. Minke inkyire w'de, Aburekyir nuhu wodzi ahaban hyihye mbuukuw m'ma woakyinkyin na wowie kyinkyin a, wodzi mbuukuw n'atutu mbre wogyi hon mfefuw enyiwa bi a? *(Replaces leaves in book, shuts it with a snap and thumps it back to its place. Sees ashes in dust-pan, takes up pan and thrusts it in Nyamikye's face).* Nsu i su a asiseev yi e?
Mpen ahin na erihwihwe m'ma m'aka akyine w'de sigyar-nsu oye ma adz'a otuw daadzi ha'i? Nnyim de Aburekyir nuhu sigyar nsu wodzi kuku *carpet* numu mbuaba bi a?

[19]

no pretty washes for their walls, I feel glad that I was not born in their days, when they lived their lives in darkness. I am particularly glad to have been born in the period when Religion had brought us refinement (...) Consider this chair, for instance. You sink into it when you sit in it, it is so pleasantly soft. It is not like the native stool, which gives you a pain in the loins when you sit on it. (...) What I cannot understand is that, in spite of all which makes our lives so enjoyable, our ancestors, whose lives seem so hard to us, lived longer and were happier than we can live or be (...) Just fancy! I do not now practise the songs I was told to sing, when I was in England (...) I have forgotten the pronounciation of the word: is it *peetal* or *pettal?* I'll consult my dictionary. *(Exit. L.)*

ashes on carpet) Wuhu ye ahumtsiw duduw! Fi ho ko!
(Exit Nyamikye, L.) Edan M'ha aye few ai! *(Looks round
admiringly)* M'ara muhwe de hen egya' num hon adan
ntwima na wodzi kukow m', na woamfa edur feefe biara
anka hon ban hu ee, nna oye m'dew de woanwo m'hon abir
du a isum agyi hen abrabo du n'. Oyem dew kesikesi de
wowu m'abir a Nyamisum dzi enyibueri aba hen man m'i.
(Sits in an easy chair.) W'ara hwe egua 'i. Eku m'a nna akehye
m' oye/tufuu/ma oye ahumka. Abegyim sasagua a eku du
a nna w'asin ye w'yew. *(Looks perplexidly at ceiling)* Dz'a
m'intzi asi nyi de ndzemba pii yi a yewo dzi sepew hen hu
ma abrabo ye ahumka n'ekyir 'i, hen mpanyinfu a nkaanu
n'hon asitsina m'ye pesee wo nhen hen enyiwa m' 'i, mbom
wonyin-i kyeri sin hen, na esu wonya asum'dwii kyen hen.
(Jumps up suddenly) E! Ndaansa 'i mimpractise endwim a
muwo Aburekyir n'wosi m' de muntu n' *(Sings falsetto)*

Snowdrops, lift your bell-like petals,
Ding! Ring! Ni _____ ng!

Mu wire efir word kur 'i mbre wobodzin: se *peetal* o: se
pettal o. Kyire munkohwe mi *diction'ry* m'. *(Exit. L.)*

*Enter Mr Brofusem L. In pyjamas and slippers. Smoking a cigar,
with newspaper in his hand.*

MR BROF I heartily curse the day my wife decided England
for a while. Ever since then, I have had nothing but we
must do this, because it is done in England, we *must* n't do
that, because it is not done by English people and so on *ad
nauseam. (Sits down, and spreads out newspaper)* It serves us
jolly well right for allowing ourselves to be dazzled by all this
flimsy foreign frippery. *(Throws away newspaper, gets up, and
walks up and down.)* The worst of it is that some of us got into
these foreign ways through no fault of our own. We were born

[21]

into a world of imitators, worse luck, ... and blind imitators, at that. They could not and cannot, distinguish cause from effect, so they have not been able to trace effect to cause, as yet. They see a thing done in England, or by somebody white; then they say we must do the same thing in Africa. It is that confounded *must* that annoys me. Why *must?* Dash it all! It becomes deuced unpleasant when it involves the sacrifice of one's comfort during the daylight hours, at least. *(Winks at the audience and laughs)* Ha! Ha! If I had not been 'cute enough to make a bargain with my wife ————By the way, you know my wife don't you? You've seen her here. You simply couldn't help seeing her, I'll wager. She jumps to the eyes, as, I think the French say. Well, as I was saying, if I had not been 'cute enough to make a bargain with my wife, my life would be perfectly miserable. You see, she says she heard in England that cigar-ashes were good for carpets. So she allows me to wear pyjamas and slippers in the house, when we have no visitors, on condition that I smoke cigars, and spread the ashes about. *(Knocks on to floor the lump of ash at end of cigar)* Rather a good idea, that, don't you think so? Fact is I like cigars. That's one of my weaknesses. You say cigars are European? Of course they are. *(Walks to extreme edge of stage)* But then, my parents set out deliberately to make me as much like a European as possible, before they sent me to England. They would have bleached my skin, if they could. I am rather glad that idiotic American hair-straightening thing did not come out in their time. I am sure they would have got me one: and I should have looked like a mad golliwog. *(Cigar goes out. He finds matches on the floor. Relights cigar, and takes a few appreciative puffs.)* I remember I was often caned for not wanting to wear boots and thick stockings. I always used to take them off when I was beyond view of the parental eye. Ha! Ha! But I must confess to my shame, that I feel hampered when I put on the native dress, because I do not know how to wear it properly: it is always slipping from my shoulder. That is why I wear pyjamas in the house: they are the freest clothing my wife will permit. Just fancy that I, a Fanti, should be able to express my thoughts better in English, because I evolved from youth-hood into manhood in England: Then, when I want now to speak my own language as much as possible, my wife compels me to speak to her always in English, since otherwise the sulks.

Enter Mrs Brofusem. L.

MRS BROF Jim!

MR BROF Yes, dear.

MRS BROF Call me "duckie". "Dear is too much common". Even some of the clerks call their wives "dear". Mrs Gush my friend at Seabourne, on the East Coast, always addressed by her husband as "duckie".

MR BROF Well, ducks?

MRS BROF Don't say "ducks". Say "duckie". Mr Gush, he always have said "duckie", not "ducks". Say "duckie", and I will call you "darling" as Mrs Gush do.

MR BROF Very good, duckie.

MRS BROF Oh, darling! You are a dear! I will kiss you.

MR BROF *(Deprecatingly)* Don'ts, I beg. The servant might see us, and what will he think? He does not understand kissing! he might think you were trying to bite me, or he might think something worse than that. You see he is a Fanti among Fantis.

MRS BROF I don't care about servant. Nobody thinks of servants thinking in England. Mrs Gush, she always kiss her husband when he extra nice. *(Embraces Mr Brofusem. They struggle)* I will kiss you.

[23]

NYAM (...) Good Lord! I'll run back. What is this I have seen?

NYAM Yes, madam.

MRS BROF (...) You intentionally came here on tip-toe. If you do that again, I shall cut down your pay. In future, knock each time you come here.

NYAM I did not think anyone was here. I thought you were on the verandah. (...) Madam, I beg your pardon. The carpet prevents one's footsteps from being heard. (...) Master ask pardon for me.

MRS BROF (...) What did you come for?

NYAM Cook want me to ask if he is to make a tart today too.

MRS BROF Yes. I have told him that if he does not serve up European sweets with any dinner he prepares, I shall dismiss him. Tell him that I told you to say that to him. (...) Very funny. Formerly, if I had neither fried nor roast plantains after meals, I felt as if I had eaten nothing. (...) O, I forget myself.

Re-enter Nyamikye, L. Walking towards door R. Sees Mr and Mrs Brofusem kissing, and stands still a moment, with mouth open.

NYAM *(Raising up his hands in surprise)* Meewoo! Kyire m'inguan Abendazi na m'ebohu'i *(Jumps back towards door, L. Mr and Mrs Brofusem spring apart, looking sheepish.)*

MRS BROF *(Recovering herself, and scowling blackly)* Nyamikye!

NYAM *(Returning)* Ewuraba. *(Avoiding her eyes)*.

MRS BROF *(Vindictively)* Ehye daara na enam denden ba ha. Eye dem bio a onu mibetsiiv w'akotua. Ekyina biara eriba ha a bo abuw m'.

NYAM M'andwin de ibiara wo ha. Midwin de gyama wowo abrendee m'. *(Kneels to Mrs Brofusem)* Ewuraba, mipa w'kyew. Adz'a otuw fam' 'i ntsirn' enam ho a wontsi w'ananadzi. *(To Mr Brofusem)* Muwura, pa kyew ma m'.

MR BROF Duckie, he is not to blame.

MRS BROF You mean I am to blame? Alright, I will never kiss you again.

MR BROF *(Aside)* What luck! *(To Mrs Brofusem)* Very good, duckie, please yourself.

MRS BROF *(To Nyamikye)* Ebeye den?

NYAM Kuku si mimbebisa w' na nde su onye *tart* n' bi a?

MRS BROF Nyew. M'asi n'de se oamfa Brofu-adokodokodzi anka edziban biara a obeye hu a onu mibeyi n'edzi, si n'de m'ara mi si w' de si n'. *(Exit Nyamikye. To Mr Brofusem)* Oye sriw ai'. *(Smiling)* Nkye nkaanu m'enya buredzikyiwii anasu esiato ampepa m'enum a nna mintsi de m'edzidzi. *(Mr Brofusem grins. Mrs Brofusem starts)* O! Muwire efir muhu. I mean to say that I have forget myself. *(Mr Brofusem laughs)* What make you laugh. *(Dabs at her eyes with a handkerchief)* You always make me ridiculous, you brute.

MR BROF *(Composing his features)* I am sorry, duckie.

MR BROF (...)

As for that Window tax affair,
we shall see!

MRS BROF *(Wiping her eyes and smiling)* Oh, how nice! I will kiss———

MR BROF *(Hurriedly)* No, thanks. I mean...er...

MRS BROF *(Bridling)* My mouth is not smell.

MR BROF *(Soothingly)* I didn't say it did.

MRS BROF Then why you say "No, thanks" in that nasty way?

MR BROF Why, didn't you say a minute ago that you would never kiss me again?

MRS BROF I didn't say it. I mean I say it because Nyamikye is here. It's English, you know, so I......

MR BROF *(Interrupting with a song)*

> Roast beef and plum-pudding
> And a glass of good beer, ———
> That's English, it's English, you know.

MRS BROF *(Looking pleased)* I like you to sing like that. It is like white man's voice.

MR BROF *(Testily)* My voice is my own. I am not an ass.

MRS BROF It is not your own voice. You told me you have train your voice when you are in England. Your voice is now English.

MR BROF Well, you *are* silly. One cannot help singing an English song, if he can sing at all, in the English manner, can he? If I sang in Fanti, although I should be singing in the same voice, the intonation would be bound to be different. Listen: *(Sings)*

> Ntokuratuw n' dama asem n'a,
> Debi ebeye dwe!
> Nto———

MRS BROF *(Looking shocked)* Oh. Jim!

MR BROF *(Surprised)* Hello, what's up?

MRS BROF How can you sing such a thing? It is only bushmen

I think the man who knocked must be in native dress. If he
were in European clothes, he would have pressed the bell.
I don't want any people in native dress to come messing up my
carpets with their dusty [bare] feet and spitting upstairs here.

and fishermen and stupids and rascals who sing that song.

MR BROF What's wrong with it? *(Yawns)* Ah————h!

MRS BROF *(Hotly)* You don't want to hear me speak. You are not polite. Mrs Gush say if a man yawns when a lady was speaking to him, his manners is shocking. It is good I returned from England the time I have come. If I was stopping only three months more, you become bushman: you have gone out in native dress when I was in England. You have eat native chop all the time I am away. Scandalous! Shocking!

MR BROF My dear—— I mean, duckie, why what have I done?

MRS BROF I do not want to hear you speak. You must be ashamed of yourself. You yawn when I speak to you. Shameful! Disgraceful!

MR BROF *(Nettled)* You know I sat up working last night till morning, because of that wretched party you would give. I should like to know how we are to keep up all this showy tomfoolery unless I work hard to earn the money you waste. I simply could'nt help yawning. If you start any married suffragette tricks with me, you will be sorry. I am getting fed up. *(Exit, L. In a rage)*.

Mrs Brofusem shrugs her shoulders, goes to the piano, and practises scales for a few moments. A knock is heard. Nyamikye enters. L, and makes for door, R.

MRS BROF Nyamikye!

NYAM Ewuraba *(Turns with hand on knob of door, R.)*

MRS BROF *(Stopping and turning round in seat)* Oye m' de myimpa a oabo abum m' n' ofura 'tam. Si n' de onkesi nuhu. *(Exit Nyamikye R.)* Ohye atar a, sin de omia *bell* n'. Minyinhwihwe tamfuranyi biara ma odzi n'ananadzi fi abeye mi *carpet* du, na oabotutuu ntefi wo mi sur. *(Goes on practising)*

NYAM It's Mr Tsiba and his daughter.
MRS BROF Show them in.

MISS TSI (...) What's this? What is she staring at me through
that glass for? Does she take me for a steamer? (...) I am well.
MR TSI (...) Speak English. Don't you understand that language?

MISS TSI I am called Araba Mansa, but my father calls me
Barbara.
MR TSI (...) Don't say "My father", say "My papa".

MR TSI (...) How do you answer when your school-mistress
calls you?

[30]

Re-enter Nyamikye. R.

NYAM Yewura Tsiba na ni ba besia n' a.

MRS BROF Oye wombra.

Exit Nyamikye. Mrs Brofusem goes up to a chair and dabs her face with a page torn from a tiny book which she hangs from her pocket. Then a handkerchief. Looks at her clothes.

MRS BROF *(Brushing her skirt with her hand)* How these ashes come here? Oh, I remember. *(Picks up lorgnette, places it on her nose and poses before glass)* That is how Mrs Gush has done it.

(Re-enter Nyamikye, R. followed by Mr Tsiba and Miss Tsiba. Nyamikye exit.)

MRS BROF Good morning, Mr Tsiba. *(Offering the tips of her fingers)* So you have brought your daughter, as you promised. How sweet of you, *(Looks at Miss Tsiba through lorgnette)* Come and shake hands, my dear. How are you?

Mr Tsiba mumbles something, confused, and grabs the whole of Mrs Brofusem's hand, bowing oddly.

MISS TSI *(Advancing to shake hands, and aside)* Na iyi e? Osi ehen nyi m' na orita m' kyikyi 'i a? *(To Mrs Brofusem)* Muhu ye.

MR TSI *(Frowning at Miss Tsiba)* Kasa Brofu: nyki etsi bi.

MRS BROF *(Sitting on a sofa)* Come and sit by me my dear. What is your name? *(To Mr Tsiba)* Please take seat.

MISS TSI Wofre m' Araba, Mansa, na m'egya onu ofre m' Barbara.

MR TSI *(Sitting)* Mma ensi "m'egya", si "mi papa".

MRS BROF Barbara! It is a fine name. Is that all, Mr Tsiba? You see in England, all fashionable young ladies get more than one Christian name.

MR TSIBA Er——yes, sir: no, er——yes——er— *(To Miss Tsiba)* Hon skur-misis fre hon a wogyi du den?

MISS TSI Yesi *"Yes ma'm"*

MR TSI *(To Mrs Brofusem)* Er——yes, ma'm. She get two names when she is baptize: Barbara Erimintrude.

MRS BROF Erimintrude. *(To herself)* I never hear that before. Fine big name, Very nice. *(To Mr Tsiba)* I will always call her Erimintrude.

MR TSIBA Thank you, sir——er——ma'm. *(Gets up)* I have bring my girl for English education.

MRS BROF Don't stand up when you are talking to me.

MR TSI Beg pardon, sir——er—ma'm. *(Gets up, then sits)* You make her behave like white lady. Teach her all the things you have learn at London. By the grace of the big one in the sky, I get some money. I have many cocoa land. I want you to make her English. She don't like stays; she don't like boots; she want to go out in native dress. She like *fufur* too much; she like *dokun* too much. I know white ladies can't chop *fufur* or dokun, because their middle is too small with stays: then she will eat nice European things. Thank you sir——er—ma'm. Ta! Ta! *(Gets up and shakes Mrs Brofusem's hand. Then says to Miss Tsiba)* Obey your new English missis. She will make you fine lady like herself. *(Turns to leave)*

MRS BROF Please, make me see you to the door. *(Walks with Mr Tsiba to door, R.)* Good-bye, Mr Tsiba. *(Exit Mr Tsiba)*.

Re-enter Mr Tsiba, R.

MR TSI Er——Mrs Brofusem, some book I have reading say, "All modest young ladies blush at certain times". I look in the dickhendry, and I see "blush" means to redden in the face", also I look "modest", and I see "chaste". I know "chaste": the minister explain this to me. But I think "blush" is some English powder for face. I have never seen it here. Order some for my daughter I have many cocoa...

MRS BROF *(Laughing)* Ah! Blush: Your daughter can't be able to blush.

MR TSI *(Offended)* You mean my daughter too raw? I say I give her to you free, gratis. Make her blush. I will pay.

MRS BROF I mean her skin don't allow it to be clear when she will blush.

MR TSI But she has fine black skin, ——velvet black. My great-grandmother he say, in old times, the blackest ladies are most beautifullest. I think my daughter's skin is alright.

MRS BROF You don't understand——

MR TSI Ma'm I went to standard seven. I understand——

MRS BROF I don't mean to say you don't understand English. How can you talk what you don't understand? You understand English but you don't know that white peoples' skin is transparent; so you can see the blood running into their faces when they are having some emotional state.

MR TSI Ah! What fine big words you use. "Transparent—— Transparent". Wait! *(Takes out a pocket Dictionary, and looks in)* Ah! Here it is: "Transparent—— that may be seen through, clear". *(To himself)* Well, my daughter's skin is clear, my skin is clear, my wife's skin is clear. We get no sickness. *(Reflects a moment)* Oh, "see through". I see! I see! Very funny. "Transparent" is like glass: no colour; so it is the blood make him red. You call that "blush". All right! Teach Barbara all the things. *(Confidentially, to Mrs Brofusem)* I can't call her Erimintrude, because it is too difficult. I see it in a book the day she is brought forth: so I call her so. *(As an afterthought)* Teach her to play nice song like the one I hear you play when I come. Thank you. *(Exit, R.)*.

Enter Nyamikye, L.

NYAM Pass chop, sah!

[33]

MRS BROF Did I not tell you the other day to say, "Lunch is on the table, madam"?

MISS TSI So you can speak Fanti! Why don't you speak it, then? If you do not let me speak Fanti, I shall run away.

MISS TSI (...) What's this? Is she a gramaphone? Well, let those who have been to England please themselves: it is not my affair. When they come back, their voices are changed into something very funny. Perhaps it is the cold that does it.

MR ONY The court has risen, I have no case tomorrow. I have taken off the European sacks and the Inns-of-court gown which are my working-clothes. I have put on the native garb, I have withdrawn my feet from boots, I have put on sandals. Now, I shall smoke awhile (...) Who is there?

MRS BROF Ewu edanu m'ansi w' de si, "*Lunch is on the table, Madam* bi a?

NYAM Dunts on table, malam. *(Exit, L)*.

MISS TSI Ana etsi Mfantsi? Oye den na enkasa 'i? Se amma m'ankasa Mfantsi a, onu mibeguan ako.

MRS BROF *(Laughing)* Come along and tidy yourself, before we go for lunch. Come on. *(Sings, Falsetto)*

"Caro—ol lo—ng, hap—p—y so—ng!
Si—ng! Si——ng! Si———ng! *(EXIT, L)*.

MISS TSI *(Following)* Na iyi e? Talking-machine a? Ose nhon ara a woako Aburekyir. Wobeba na hon ndzi adan aye srisrisriw. Gyema awow n'a.

SCENE TWO

Mr Onyimdzi's Smoking-room.

MR ONY *(Dropping into a chair)* M'apun *court;* ekyina su minnyi asem dzi-m'apupor Brofu nkotoku na *Inns of court* kramo a woye m'edwuma-ntar n'egu. m'efura 'tam; m'eyi m'anan ofi aaupatsir m'; M'ahye mpabua. Nkyi mubonum ebua kakra. *(A knock is heard)* Who is there?

Enter Half-crown.

MR ONY Well, Half-crown?

HALF Some man day, sah.

MR ONY What kind man?

MR ONY I thank you, sir. Please sit.

MR ONY Who told you that I wanted a clerk?

MR ONY Look here, do you understand Fanti? If so speak
Fanti. Why did you leave Chutney's store?

MR OK The white man kicked me, and I called him "white
savage".

MR ONY Ha! Ha! Was it the white man called Ipay?

MR OK Yes, sir.

MR ONY Was that why he dismissed you? Are you a son of
Mr Okadu, the carpenter.

MR OK Yes sir.

MR ONY How much do you think you are worth?

HALF 'E get plenty fine clo'es, big collar, boots shine all same glass. 'E shine for true.

MR ONY Lawyer or big man?

HALF No, sah. 'E no big man, sah. I see 'im for Chutney & Co.

MR ONY Clerk, eh? Well, whoever it is, it's jolly rotten of him to come bothering me when I am going to have a quiet smoke. Where the devil is he?

HALF Ou'side, sah.

MR ONY All right; tell him say come.

HALF Yas, sah. *(Exit Half-crown)*

Enter Mr Okadu, very bashful.

MR OK Good afternoon, sir!

MR ONY Ya ewura! Ku ho.

MR OK *(Sitting on the edge of a chair)* I want you to teach me to be English, sir. I will be your clerk, and take no pay, sir.

MR ONY Wana si w' de muruhwihwe krakyi?

MR OK I think since you have win many case, you will want another clerk soon.

MR ONY Nhwe, ana etsi M'fantsi a? Se etsi a, onu kasa Mfantsi. Abenadzi 'ntsir na ifi *Chutney* fiadsi 'i?

MR OK Burenyi n' wo m' intsia, mna mifre n' *white savage*.

MR ONY Ha! Ha! Burenyi n' a wofre n' Ipay n' a?

MR OK Nyew.

MR ONY Iyi 'ntsir na oyi w'edzi yi a? Egya Okadu, *carpenternyi* n' ni ba nyi w' a?

MR OK Nyew.

MR ONY Eben akotua na edwin de ofata w'?

MR OK I don't want anything, sir. My mother gives me everything I want. I think if you will teach me some European things to make me like a white man, I will not take any money.

MR ONY What do you mean?

[37]

MR OK I mean to say that I have no money to go to England like you. So I want to beg you to train me. I like Miss Tsiba, and I want to marry her. But her father will not be consent unless he know I am with somebody like you who has gone England. She has been took to living with Mrs Brofusem, and she is becoming very smart, so I want to be smart, too, sir.

MR ONY By Jove, you are getting too wise for your years: So you want to get round the old man? All right, come to my office tomorrow.

MR OK All right sir. Thank you sir. Good afternoon sir. *(Exit)*.

MR ONY Good afternoon! *(Walking to the extreme edge of the stage)* By Jove, I will have some fun with that numskull. *(A knock is heard)* Well?

Enter Half-crown with two visiting-cards.

HALF Two man come gi' me dem book say make I gi' you.

MR ONY *(Taking cards)* You *are* droll. Two *man*, you say? Why, they are ladies; show them in at once. *(Exit Half-crown)* It's the old Gorgon and a victim. Poor "devil-ess"! Wonder what's the game?

Enter Mrs Brofusem and Miss Tsiba.

MR ONY How d'you do, Mrs. Brofusem? Take a seat, please.

MRS BROF I really must apologise for my rudeness *(Touching Mr Onyimdzi's finger-tips with her finger-tips)* I ought to call long ago. Now I have to take Miss Tsiba *(Presenting Miss Tsiba)* round to see my friends. So, to kill one bird with two stones, I have returned your call, and at the same time introducing Miss Tsiba to you.

MR ONY *(Shaking hands with Miss Tsiba)* Pleased to meet you, Miss Tsiba.

MISS TSIBA *(Bashfully)* I am very well, thank you sir.

MR ONY Please excuse me one minute. *(Goes to the door and*

turns round) Half-crown! Oh, here you are. Go to Chutney's and say "Port wine". Then go to them mami who make cake; buy some. There's money. *(Closes door, and turns round)* I am afraid Miss Tsiba is shy: don't you think so, Mrs Brofusem? I think she would feel more at home if we spoke Fanti. *(Album from a shelf, and hands it to Miss Tsiba).* Look at the pictures in this album; they may interest you: they are views of places I visited in England.

MRS BROF Of course, she is shy; all our girls are. Accra girls are better: they speak English like English ladies.

MR ONY *(Aside)* That's news.

MRS BROF But I must say it will be good for some Accra girls to be shy. Did you ever visit Seabourne, in Blankshire?

MR ONY Seabourne? Seabourne? Oh! on the East coast? I believe I was there one week-end.

MRS BROF What did you think of the Pier Pavilion?

MR ONY I liked it; the entertainments there were splendid.

MRS BROF I wish we have a place like that in this country. You must help us when we start to make concerts and bazaars, in order to collecting money to build a Pier Pavilion here. Of course the voices of our girls wants training; but that is matter of time. I think we can manage to get some girls to serve as waitresses in cap and apron and collar and cuffs. The girls in the place gets nothing to do to keep them out of mischief when they left school.

MR ONY I used to wonder why some of them did not go in for typing.

MRS BROF I think typing is good: it would be like England. Then we know where the get the money to buy all the pretty clothes they wear.

MR ONY On the whole, I should think, the girls would be better off if they just stuck to sewing and other forms of womanly employment. They should at least know how to cook: it is

MRS ONY (…) There are those who think pig's entrails a delicacy.

more important than embroidering or doing drawn-thread work.

MRS BROF I hope, Mr Onyimdzi, you do not think that you would like your wife to go to the kitchen.

MR ONY O dear no: such a thing simply could'nt enter my head; fact is, I do not intend to marry.

MRS BROF You mean here, I suppose. I expect you get nice white girl in your sleeve.

MR ONY White girl? No thanks! I do not want any such thing as a wife. Of course, if I wanted to marry, I should marry here. I do not see the sense in bringing out a white girl, when one can marry here. What one should bring from Europe is what he has got into the habit of considering essential to his well-being. Personally, I think a white girl would blight my life: for one thing, I should never get used to her.

MRS BROF Funny! I meet, when I was in England, many young men who will give very much to marry a white girl.

MR ONY Well, "Every man to his taste", as the French say. We say here: "Ibi n'akondodzi nyi dompo ni nsun".

MRS BROF Well, I am surprise! Fancy being able to talk Fanti like that, when you have spend many years in England. How can you remember? Most young men don't able to understand vernacular when they return from England.

MR ONY You see, I always communed with myself in Fanti, even when I was at College. And as I did not care much for the company of the white fellows, I had plenty of time to keep up my Fanti. But sometimes I find it easier to speak English, and I slip into it unawares when I am speaking Fanti, at such times. As a rule, when I am angry, or more than ordinarily perturbed, I find myself either speaking or brooding in English when my peace of mind is restored. At other times, it is the other way about. I suppose that is to be expected of us social hybrids, born into one race,

[41]

and brought up to live like members of another race.*

Enter Half-crown. Takes up small table, and places it between Mrs Brofusem and Miss Tsiba. Goes out and brings tray. Sets out a plate of cake three wine-glasses, wine in a decanter, and a tin of chocolates. Draws a chair to Mr Onyimdzi's seat, Goes out and brings another tray, From which he sets out a plate of buredzi tutui, *a plate of* nkatsi kyiwii *and a finger-bowl filled with water upon chair. Then exit Half-crown.*

MR ONY *(To Mrs Brofusem, filling a wine-glass)* May I?

MRS BROF Thanks!

MR ONY *(To Miss Tsiba, filling another wine-glass)* May I?

MISS TSI No, thank you! If it is port, I do not like it: it smells like Elexir.

MRS BROF Oh, Erimintrude!

MR ONY *(Aside)* Good heavens, what a name! I suppose she wanted to say "Ermyntrude". *(To Miss Tsiba)* Well, I shan't press you; but won't you try a piece of cake or a chocolate, or some *buredzi tutui?*

MISS TSI I think I will take *buredzi tutui.*

MR ONY Please do. Here is a finger-bowl for you. *(Raising his voice)* Half-crown! *(Enter Half-crown)* Bring another finger bowl *(Pointing to the finger-bowl. Exit Half-crown.)*

MRS BROF Do behave, Erimintrude. A cake is more genteel ...than *buredzi tutui.* Or else, take a chocolate. I recommend creamy ones. All young ladies in England chop creamy chocolates.

MR ONY I am afraid there is none in this tin: they are all more or less hard.

MISS TSI Never mind. I do not like creamy chocolates. When the thing inside come for your tongue, it is like eating cock-

---

* These arguments appear verbatim in Sekyi's *The Meaning of the Expression 'Thinking in English'.* (1937) (Editor's note).

[42]

roaches or beetles. When you walk on them something white co——

MRS BROF *(Very loudly)* Oh, Erimintrude!

Miss Tsiba jumps in her seat, and knocks over the chocolate tin. Re-enter Half-crown with another finger-bowl, which he places on chair by Mr Onymdzi.

MISS TSI I am very sorry. I beg pardon.

MRS BROF You ought to be shamed of yourself.

MR ONY Please don't: it's nothing. Half-crown, pick them thing for ground. *(Half-crown obeys, and exit to Mrs Brofusem)* I shall join you in a glass of wine. *(Both drink)* I seldom take these things though: I prefer *ahe* myself.

MRS BROF You are very odd Mr Onyimdzi. *Ahe!* The idea! Why only fishermen's wives drink that.

MR ONY None the less, I like it. It's a fine drink. *(To Miss Tsiba)* Do take some buredzi, if you prefer that. I always have a plate in lieu of afternoon tea.

MRS BROF You are very funny, Mr Onyimdzi. *(Rising after a pause)* We must go now. Don't forget to come to my "At Home" on Saturday. You know, Saturday is my "At Home" day. I will send you card. Good afternoon, Mr Onyimdzi!

MISS TSI Good afternoon, sir! *(Following Mrs Brofusem)*.

MR ONY Let me see you to the door.

(Exeunt all three. Re-enter Mr Onyimdzi, after a few moments.)

MR ONY So that's the girl Okadu is sweet on. She is rather charming: she is fresh and decidedly frank. It is a pity old Mrs B. has got her in tow. I am afraid the dear girl will be metamorphosed into an idiotic, conceited, simpering piece of femininity in a short while. It's a funny world: those who are warm, natural and unconstrained are reckoned barbarous: those who are cold, artificial, and confoundedly formal are regarded as refined.

[43]

MR ONY (...) Just look at them. That is the sort of thing they
like. It is becoming chronic with them to care only for such
things. They say there will be some games played. I have an
idea they will play such European games as Tennis and
Croquet and Aunt Sally etc. Wait! I shall ask Mrs Brofusem
to let the young ladies play *ampe*, and observe her reply.

MR ONY Look here, why don't you speak Fanti? Why so much
English?

[ACT TWO]

SCENE ONE
*A Garden-Party at Victoria Park.**

Ladies and Gentlemen, in European clothes, parading up and down in the background, chatting and laughing. Enter L. Mr Onyimdzi, in native dress.

MR ONY *(Looking at the crowd)* Wonhwe hon. Dz'a wope ara nyi n'. Oriye aka hon du. Wosi wobedzi agur. Biribi susu mu du de croquet na tennis na Aunt Sally na Aburofugur a otstsi dem na wobedzi. Twen! Impire mibesi Mrs Brofusem de oma nkataesia n' nezi ampe, na m'ahwe dz'a obeka.

Enter Mr Okadu, R, Passes Mrs Brofusem and Miss Tsiba. Makes as if to salute them. They cut him, and pass haughtily by.

MR ONY   By Jove! Miss Tsiba has got it badly, poor girl. What confounded side! Hello, Okadu!

MR OK She would not look at me.

MR ONY Of course she wouldn't. Seeing that the old girl was in charge of her. Don't you see she has probably told her that in England fashionable ladies bow first to gentlemen whom they care to recognize, before the gentleman salute them.

MR OK I will remember next time, sir. I have learnt the rules you gave me, sir.

MR ONY Wusu nkasa Mfantsi. Brofu pi yi e?

---

* Victoria Park, Cape Coast.

[45]

MR OK Why, sir, this is garden-party, sir ——English idea. We must talk English, sir.

MR ONY Oh, alright, please yourself. Well, what rules were you talking about?

MR OK The instructions you gave me as to how I am to behave here, sir.

MR ONY Oh, I see. *(Aside)* By Jove, I forgot all about it. We shall have some fun, I promise you. *(To Mr Okadu)* Now, you remember what I said? Miss Tsiba seems to have been well primed by Mrs Brofusem. She will not talk to you because you have not been introduced to her. You say you want to make her acquaintance without Mrs Brofusem's knowing anything about it. Well, one way in which you can do it is by knocking away her parasol, if you are lucky enough to find her by herself. Then you should pick up the parasol, and politely present it to her, with profuse apologies. You understand? Don't go and muddle it.

MR OK Yes sir.

MR ONY I mean knocking it away as if by accident.

MR OK I know, sir.

MR ONY Well, I'm off now. I shall try to get Mrs. Brofusem out of the way. Then I leave it to you to go in and win——or muff it.

MR OK I can do it alright, sir. *(Exit Mr Onyimdzi)*.

Mr Okadu draws up a chair, sits, and takes out of his pocket a small looking-glass, a piece of chalk, and his handkerchief. Chalks his face, and regards himself in the glass with satisfaction. Then gets up, flaps the chalk out of his handkerchief, and walks up and down.

MR OK

A product of the Low School, embroidered by the High,
Upbrought and trained by similar products, here am I.
I speak English to soften my harsher native tongue:

It matters not if often I speak the Fanti wrong.

I'm learning to be British and treat with due contempt
The worship of the fetish, from which I am exempt.

I was baptized an infant——a Christian hedged around,
With prayer from the moment my being was unbound.

I'm clad in coat and trousers, with boots upon my feet;
And *tamfurafu** and Hausas I seldom deign to greet:

For I despise the native that wears the native dress—
The badge that marks the bushman, who never will
[progress.

All native ways are silly, repulsive, unrefined.
All customs superstitious, that rule the savage mind.

I like Civilization, and I'd be glad to see
All people that are pagan eschew idolatry.

I reckon high the power of governors and such;
But our own Kings and Chiefs, —why, *they* do not
[matter much.

And so you see how loyal a Britisher I've grown——
How very proud and zealous a subject of the Crown.

I wish I'd go to England, where, I've been often told,
No filth and nothing nasty you ever may behold:
And there I'll try my hardest to learn the English life;
And I shall try to marry a real English wife.†

Enter one Lady from the crowd.

LADY *(To Mr Okadu)* Come and play some game. *(Rejoins the crowd).*

MR OK I don't want games.

Enter another Lady from the crowd.

---

* People who wear "native" dress.
† Cf. Sekyi's long poem 'The Sojourner', where these lines originally
   appeared (Editor's Note).

[47]

MR OK Oh go away!

LADY *(To Mr Okadu)* It left one man to play doubles for tennis. *(Rejoins the crowd).*

MR OK Fi nuhu!

LADIES & GENTLEMEN To the games! The games! *(Exeunt).*

Enter Mrs Brofusem and Miss Tsiba.

MRS BROF Now Erimintrude, you say you have a headache. It is a pity. I was going to see you take part in croquet tournament. Sit here, and cover yourself with your umbrella. I'll be back soon. *(Exit).*

MR OK Aha— There she is!

MISS TSI Oh. There is that young man who look too much at me at Chapel last Sunday. He look fine. I think I have seen him coming out of Mr. Onyimdzi's house the day we have called there. Oh, he is coming here! I hope he will want to speak to me. I will drop my handkerchief when he gets near; then he pick it up, and we can talk without being introduction. That's what the girl has done in the book I read last night till morning.

MR OK *(Walking slyly towards Miss Tsiba)* Oh, I feel nervous! I wonder if I can able to manage it. Ah——h! I will fall down *(Slips intentionally behind Miss Tsiba's chair, and then clutches the top of her parasol as if to save himself).*

MISS TSI *(Jumping up)* Whatever is that? *(Turns round)* Oh, I hope you dont hurt yourself.

MR OK *(Jumping up with alacrity, and raising his hat with a flourish)* Please pardon my clumsiness: I slipped just behind your chair. Allow me to restore to you your umbrella. *(Brushing sunshade and handing it).*

MISS TSI *(Receiving sunshade)* Thank you very much. You are kind. I hope you have not hurt.

MR OK I am all right, thank you; but I am glad I fell down.

MISS TSI What you mean?

1ST LADY What fine clothes she wears!
2ND LADY Just look at her parasol.
3RD LADY Just look at her shoes!

4TH LADY I prefer her spectacles (lorgnette).

MR OK I mean to say that I am glad I have fell, because it has introduced us.

MISS TSI *(Aside)* He is nice, he knows many things: Mr Onyimdzi has taught him.

MR OK Please walk with me.

MISS TSI All right. *(Exeunt Miss Tsiba and Mr Okadu. Enter Mrs Brofusem.)*

MRS BROF *(Looking round)* I wonder where she's got to. Perhaps she has gone to drink tea. She has wake up now: but it was difficult to make her of anything.

Enter several ladies who crowd admiringly round Mrs Brofusem.

1ST LADY N'atar 'i ye fe ai!

2ND LADY Nhwe ni kyim!

3RD LADY Nhwe n'asupatsir!

Mrs Brofusem regards ladies through her lorgnette.

4TH LADY Emi n'ahwihwe-enyiwa n' na mi pe.

MRS BROF *(Pleased)* Ah! Bring chairs, and let us talk.

LADIES ALL Yes! We want to talk: tell us about England.

MRS BROF

I'm glad I've been to England,
And seen her many sights,
And had the chance to taste and
    Enjoy her sweet delights.

I'm glad I've been to England.
    My eyes are open now:
I hate our sluggish life and
    Our simple wants, I vow.

I'm glad I've been to England.
    All my surroundings would
I quickly anglicize, and
    Re-model as I should.

[51]

I'm glad I've been to England:
    Behold me spick and span
In silk and patent shoes, and
    With parasol and fan.

I'm glad I've been to England,
    And learned to rule my spouse:
For there the wives are bold, and
    Command in every house.

I'm glad I've been to England,
    Where I have learnt to make
Sweet dainty things like tarts and
    Blanc-mange and fairy-cake.

Had I not been to England,
    I'd be at home, all day
House-keeping with my maids, and
    With little time to play.

But now I've been to England,
    Where ladies oft are out,
I like to call on friends, and
    With them, to gad about.

Ladies applaud wildly, nodding approval at the end of each line.

MRS BROF Let's go and see the young people play games. That foolish young man Mr Onyimdzi, say that we must play *ampé*. The idea! *Ampé* for ladies in European clothes! He must be mad or drunk.
(Exeunt Mrs Brofusem and Ladies).

Enter Mr Onyimdzi. Sees a bevy of young ladies making for him.

MR ONY Good lord! I'm in for it. I can stand the sober ones a little; but these giddy ones absolutely get on my nerves. It's like their bally cheek to come bothering me.

GIRLS ALL *(Crowding round Mr Onyimdzi)* Oh, where is Mrs Brofusem?

MR ONY I am afraid I don't know. I saw her somewhere a little while ago. I forget where: perhaps in the refreshment tent.

GIRLS ALL *(Bringing chairs, and forcing Mr Onyimdzi into one)* Do sit down, Mr Onyimdzi. We will ask you some questions. Don't you like English things? Why do you wear native dress? We all want you to wear English clothes: you will look very nice The native dress don't able to cover your right shoulder, so it is naked: it is not nice.

MR ONY I suppose you mean 'bare'. There is a great difference between nakedness and bareness.

GIRLS ALL But Mrs Brofusem says it is indecent if any part of your body is naked, except your face and neck, and breast when you wear evening-dress. So we have to wear gloves and mittens; besides, we must powder our face.

MR ONY That's all nonsense. Mrs Brofusem does not know everything.

GIRLS ALL Why she has gone to England, so she can't do anything wrong.

We follow Mrs Brofusem,
    Who is so nice, you know;
We like her ways, we'll follow them ——

MR ONY *(Interrupting)* Because they're loud and low.

GIRLS ALL Oh, don't do that!

She dresses up so very well,
    And walks with such an air,
And her "At Homes" are very swell——

MR ONY *(Interrupting again)* And vulgar, I declare.

GIRLS ALL Oh, don't do that!

We want to be like her, and walk
    Like English ladies do.
And sing like her, and laugh, and talk——

[53]

1ST GIRL So you mean to stick to the native dress. If ——

1ST GIRL What do you take yourself to be? Do you think, you who only learnt to walk in boots the other day, that you are better than I? If you like, let us walk together: do you think you are my equal?

3RD GIRL Adwua, don't ——

1ST GIRL Pooh! Do you call yourself a "frock lady"?

* In mss. the following is substituted: "There are high and low grades of people in England. Mrs Brofusem certainly does remind me of one of one of these grades, but I will not say which." Then square brackets begin.

[54]

MR ONY *(Interrupting again)* As if you had the 'flu.

GIRLS ALL Oh, Mr Onyimdzi, you will make us angry. Perhaps you hate Mrs Brofusem. Why? She ought to remind you of England.

MR ONY I should think she does. You see, in England, there are the real "upper ten', then the parvenu 'upper ten", the contented middle-class, the socially ambitious middle-class, the——

*[1ST GIRL Do the middle-class live in tents? You have say the "un-tented middle-class".

MR ONY No I said 'the contented middle-class'.

GIRLS ALL We have all hear you say "untented". You never like to know you are wrong.

1ST GIRL *(Digging into Mr Onymedzi's ribs with her parasol)* Ye ewu si etam ana na ibofura. Se——

2ND GIRL Don't talk Fanti: we are ladies.

1ST GIRL Na iyi su e? Edaansa 'i ara a *irisuasua* asupatsir m'nantsiw 'i su, edwin de nde aye yie asin m'. Epe a suer ma yenantsiw. Edwin de enyi m'se a?

3RD GIRL Adwua, mma nye—I mean Jane, don't be unladylike.

1ST GIRL You unladylike yourself. You unladylike yourself. *(Gets up and leaves the rest of the girls)*.

MR ONY Now, what's the matter? Miss Akuma, please come back: the crowd in the street is looking at you.

1st girl comes back, and draws her chair a little apart from the rest.

2ND GIRL Of course, you only went to form four.

1ST GIRL Hyia– Efre wu hu abiraba?

MR ONY Please, don't quarrel. I was talking about the English classes: You did not allow me to add that there were also the steady working-classes, the discontented working-classes and the people of the slums.

1ST GIRL You are imitating me, aren't you?

3RD GIRL You are too silly.

1ST GIRL Your clothes do not suit you.

3RD GIRL Your conduct does not suit your clothes.

1ST & 3RD GIRLS What has that to do with you?

5TH GIRL You may go, for all I care.

4TH GIRL Classes? Have they got leaders? And do they meet every week and pray and tell feelings?

MR ONY I mean grades of people ——social grades.

4TH GIRL Like 'high grade' at school?

MR ONY Exactly. You see, some of the grades are high, whilst others are disgustingly low. Mrs Brofusem reminds me of one of these classes, but I will not say which.

5TH GIRL But Mrs Brofusem is high: she has gone England.

MR ONY All right. Have it your own way. I must say, though, that there are many people who have never set foot out of this country, who are worth ten thousand of those who have lived in some White-man's-land or other.

1ST & 3RD Not so. *(They glare at each other)*.

1ST & 3RD GIRLS Not so. *(They glare at each other)*.

MR ONY Oh, yes, that is so. Those of our genuine Fanti old men who are proud in every way of their nationality are wiser, healthier, and infinitely more respectable and dignified than those who are anglicized.

1ST & 3RD GIRLS Not so.

1ST GIRL *(To 3rd Girl)* Ye irisuasua m'nta?

3RD GIRL *(To 1st Girl)* Eye adzi gyingyan duduw.

1ST GIRL W'atar mfata w'.

3RD GIRL W'abrabo mfata atar.

5TH GIRL Why, you talking vernacular. That is unladylike.

MR ONY Hello! What's happened now?

1ST & 3RD GIRLS *(To 5th Girl)* Oye wu hu asem a? *(They get up and exeunt separately).*

5TH GIRL Wonko ara su!

REM GIRLS *(Jumping up heatedly, and gesticulating in Mr Onyimdzi's face)* We know how to behave: we have read "*Don't*".

MR ONY But *now* you are misbehaving.

2ND GIRL You don't behave yourself. Look at your cloth: it is savage.

4TH GIRL Yes. You have English education, yet you wear cloth. Don't you misbehave, then?

5TH GIRL You are not lawyer if you do not go England.

6TH GIRL Yes. You do not behave yourself: you come to garden-party in native dress.

MR ONY Dear me! What a hornets' nest I have upset about my ears! Now ladies, look at the——

REM GIRLS No! No! No! We will look nothing. You abuse us.

MR ONY The crowd in the street is highly amused by this bit of comedy. Let us be friends again. I'll answer any questions you ask.

REM GIRLS *(Reseating themselves, Mr Onyimdzi also doing so)* All right.

MR ONY You say I ought not to wear native dress, because I have studied in England, under English teachers?

REM GIRLS Yes! Yes! You have English education.

MR ONY But to study in England is not the same as to have an English education.

REM GIRLS Mrs Brofusem says that you have English education. So you must use English things.

MR ONY But I am Fanti——born here, brought up here till I was about seventeen, before I was sent to England.

REM GIRLS It does n't matter. If you are in England, you must do like Englishman.

MR ONY Except where such conduct will distort the self in you. There are several things English people do just because they have unconsciously got into the way of doing them. Such things, among each people, are never capable of being learnt. If anyone attemps to learn them, he becomes ludicrous in the extreme.

REM GIRLS But you do not answer our question. Is not your education English?

MR ONY It is mixed. I believe, at school here, I was more anglicized than I became after I had lived six months in England. By the time I finished my course, I found I had become a Fanti man who had studied and thought in England, rather than an anglicized Fanti, or a bleached Negro.

REM GIRLS Don't say 'Negro', say 'coloured man'.

MR ONY I am not a coloured man: I am a Negro.

REM GIRLS All right. But if the English are not here, you will not be educated. You must thank them for that.

MR ONY There is no necessity for such thanks. They came here of their own free will, and tampered with our national life. You see, education is no more nor less than the training of the young, in each community, to take their places as useful members of their respective communities. The system of education is simple or complex, and the period of tutelage short or long, according as the life of the people whose children are to be brought up is natural or artificial.

REM GIRLS We do not understand that. You mean to say you are not glad that you are educated?

MR ONY I mean I am sorry I am civilized.

REM GIRLS Then you are sorry you have education.

MR ONY That does not follow. To be educated to civilization is unfortunate; to be educated to the natural way of living is a blessing.

REM GIRLS You mean civilization is bad?

MR ONY Most certainly. To be civilized is to be made effeminate: your wants increase, and your contentment decreases in proportion. The civilized man is a product of man's discontent; but the student of Nature, the truly observant thinker, is one of the most beautiful flowers in Nature's Garden.]*

* Passage in square brackets ends. See above p. 55 footnote for beginning of passage, the whole of which could be omitted, if so desired.

REM GIRLS You talk things we cannot understand. Why are you lawyer?

MR ONY Because there is established here an English law-court for natives.

REM GIRLS No! Because you want to get rich quick.

MR ONY You are wrong there. If I had wanted to get rich quick, as you put it, I should have become a cocoa-man, or else an owner of lorries.

REM GIRLS Yes. You are lawyer because you want to get rich quick. We know your tricks; Mrs Brofusem told us that you like to fool other people, so that you alone know many European things.

MR ONY Mrs Brofusem is a silly woman.

REM GIRLS *(Getting up in a rage, and shaking their parasols at Mr Onyimdzi)* How dare you, you and your cloth? Mrs Brofusem is not a woman, and she is not silly: she is a fine lady.

MR ONY Exactly. The lady in her is quite microscopic.

Enter Mr Okadu, very much excited. Is intercepted by Girls when making for Mr Onyimdzi.

REM GIRLS Oh, Mr Okadu, have you seen Mrs Brofusem?

MR OK Yes. She sit looking the croquet.

REM GIRLS Good-bye, naughty Mr Onyimdzi. Good-bye Mr Okadu. *(Exeunt).*

MR OK *(Rushing to Mr Onyimdzi)* Please, sir, congratulate me.

MR ONY Congratulate you? What on earth for?

MR OK I thought you said, in England, people who are engaged are congratulated.

MR ONY But you are not engaged, are you?

MR OK Of course, yes, sir. I am engaged to Miss Tsiba.

MR ONY What!

MR OK True, sir: I am engaged to Miss Tsiba.

MR ONY How did you manage it? It is rather quick work, you know.

MR TSI O, Where are the knife and fork?

BOY They are here.

MR TSI Why did you not place them on the table?

BOY You said the other day, that you could not enjoy your food when you used them.

MR TSI Bring them. (...) What else can we do? I suppose we have to use them.

MR OK We are both reading the same book, sir. We read it
last night, till morning. The chief woman in the book, she
drop her handkerchief. The chief man in the book pick it up,
and give it to the girl. Then they fall in love at first sight.
Then they get engaged.

MR ONY Really, I hope you are joking. People don't get
engaged in that lightning way hereabouts. Her people may
object, —— and yours, for that matter.

MR OK But we are engaged English fashion, sir. Her father
like English things, and Mrs Brofusem will be very glad,
and make her father consent.

MR ONY I honestly hope you are joking. If not, I am sorry
I had anything to do with it. The native custom must be
observed. If you really love the girl, get engaged to her in the
proper way. Otherwise you will both be very sorry for it.

SCENE TWO

Mr Tsiba's Asa. Doors R. C. & L. Cupboard L.

*Mr Tsiba, in native dress, cloth lowered to waist, seated at a table
laden with native food in nkwansan and plates. Boy waiting.
Mr Tsiba washes his hands, and eats native fashion, for some
minutes. Then he regards his right hand.*

MR TSI O! Sikan na faka n' wo hin?

BOY Wo wo ha. *(Taking them from cupboard).*

MR TSI Abenadzi 'ntsir na amfa antuw pun 'i?

BOY Edanu esi edzi dzidzi a emmii.

MR TSI Fa bra. *(Aside)* Na yeriye n' den? Dzidzi ara na yedzi
bedzidzi. (Washes his hands and wipes them).

[63]

NNA SU Here is what you asked me to prepare for you. Ever
  since I was born, I have never seen bananas sliced and fried.

MR TSI Let me see.

NNA SU Here it is.

MR TSI Pooh! You will never be any good at anything. Didn't
  you hear what Mansa said, when she was here, the other day?
  She said flour, eggs, butter and milk had to be mixed with it.

NNA SU Is it a European confection?

MR TSI Yes. It is called "fruiters" (i.e. fritters).

NNA SU *You* called it "fried bananas". Very good. I shall make
  particular enquiries about it when Araba comes again.

MR TSI Kofi see who it is. (...) Hide the food in the cupboard.

BOY It's Mrs Brofusem and Mr Okadu's son — the one in
  Lawyer Onyuldzi's office.

MR TSI (...) Very good (...) when they come, tell them that
  I shall be with them presently.

NNA SUMPA I thank you, Madam, I thank you, Sir. Kofi, tell
  your papa that he has visitors (...) Please sit.

MR TSI I wish [you]... er.

Enter Nna Sumpa with covered plate.

NNA SU Adz'a esi minye n' na midzi aba 'i. Mi na wu m' ara a owu m' munhun impua a wotwitwa kyiw da.

MR TSI Ma munhwe.

NNA SU Onu nyi *(Shows contents).*

MR TSI Hyiepo! Inkahu biribiara ye da! Mansa ba ha edanu 'i a oke 'i antsi? Ode wodzi isem na kyirefua na buter na mirkyi fura m'.

NNA SU Brofu-'dziban a?

MR TSI Nyew Wofre n' "frutes".

NNA SU Ewu efre n' "Mpua kyiwii". Oye. Araba ba bio a onu mi bebisa n' mu yie.

A knock is heard.

MR TSI Kofi, kohwe se wana a. *(Exit Boy. Hurriedly, to wife)* Yiyi edziban n'kosuma koba n'm'.

Re-enter Boy R.

BOY Mami Mrs Brofusem na onyi Papa Okadu ni ba n' a owo Lawyer Onyimdzi n'office n'a.

MR TSI *(Jumping up excitedly)* Oye. *(To wife)* Wo ba a, si hon de miriba *(Exit C)*

Enter Mrs Brofusem and Mr Okadu.

MRS BROF *(Looking through lorgnette)* How d'ee du, Madam Sumpa? *(Shakes hands superciliously with Nna Sumpa)*

MR OK Morning, Madam Sumpa.

NNA SUMPA Y'ewura-yir! Y'ewura! Muwara wo dan m'. Kofi, kesi wu papa de nyimpa aba ha. *(Exit Boy)* Wonkuku fa m'. *(Dusts two chairs, and brings them forward).*

Enter Mr Tsiba in European clothes (pyjamas).

MR TSI Mima ——er — Good afternoon, Mrs Brofusem! *(Shakes finger-tips).*

MRS BROF Good afternoon! I have bring you good news.

MR TSI Good news? Anybody want cocoa-land to buy?

MRS BROF Oh no! Not that kind of good news. It's about your daughter: Mr Okadu *(Presenting Mr Okadu)* and she are engaged.

MR TSI Engaged to do what?

MRS BROF To be marriage, of course.

MR TSI What! I don't know anything about it. *(Glowers at Mr Okadu)* He lie.

MRS BROF Mr Tsiba, you don't ——

MR TSI Yes I do. *(Rushes at Mr Okadu, who moves quickly backward till sharply stopped by wall)* Who gave you my daughter? Liar! Scorpion!

MRS BROF But they have engaged in English fashion.

MR TSI *(Aghast)* What!

MRS BROF In England, the young people get engaged first, and break it to their parents afterwards.

MR TSI *(Hopefully)* Break the engagement?

MRS BROF No: the happy news.

MR TSI *(Disappointed)* Oh! So, in England, the news that your daughter has dashed herself to a men is good news? And they spend so much money on she-male education?

MRS BROF Yes.

MR TSI Then it must be good. I didn't know that before.

MRS BROF Yes. I know you didn't know. That is why I brought Mr Okadu to you. You see, we want to be English. Mr Okadu is almost a white man. *(Mr Okadu tries to look white)*. He has been with Mr Onyimdzi.

MR TSI Lawyer Onyimdzi, the one who wear English clothes for court and office, and wear native dress when at home and when going to see his friends? I don't like him. Only when he talk you know he has gone England: he don't do fine things like other men who have gone England.

MR TSI (...) Why should I give money to the man who wants to marry my daughter? Do people suppose I am afraid no one will marry her?

MRS BROF Ah! But you did not see him when he was in England. He was always very smart: he get velvet collar on his overcoat. He never like to hear me say that. He says he is only neat in his clothing when he is in England.

MR TSI Velvet collar! He must be fine gentlemen, then. But why he like native dress so much?

MRS BROF I can't able to comprehend that myself. Now, call Mr Okadu to kneel before you, and kiss his forehead.

MR TSI *(Aghast)* Kiss him! He will slap my face. I read the other day that white men kiss their wives. So, yesterday next, I try to kiss my wife: but she scratch my face, and say I am drunk.

MRS BROF But in England, future fathers-in-law kiss their future sons-in-law on the forehead.

MR TSI I will do it, then. *(To Mr Okadu)* Come and kneel. *(Mr Okadu obeys reluctantly)* Look, Mrs Brofusem. *(Lightly touches Mr Okadu's forehead with tightly closed lips, and wipes his mouth vigorously).*

MR OK I want to marry your daughter soon.

MR TSI Soon? But you must order things from England. If you make them here, the wedding will not be grand. Order things from England, Also have lorry-wedding.

MRS BROF But that is not right.

MR TSI ⎱ What is not right?
MR OK ⎰

MRS BROF In England, it is the bride's father who give clothes to the bride. Some of them even give much money to the girl to take to the man.

MR TSI No! No! That is not very nice. Woyenden Su na se ibi ribewar mi ba a midzi dwetee bema benyin n' e? Wo si musuro de onkenya kun a?

MRS BROF No, but it is done in England.

MR TSI I beg you: I forgotten.

[69]

MR TSI (…) Akosua, this young man is going to marry Barbara: he is going to have a wedding.

NNA SU Is he engaged to her? What strange news is this?

MR TSI Yes, he is engaged to her.

NNA SU How is it I was not told when she was engaged?

MR TSI It was done in the English manner.

NNA SUMPA Nobody has asked my daughter in marriage: nobody has come to pay the earnest money for engagements. If you allow my daughter to be fooled*, you will find out something new about my temper. Since I married you I have never disobeyed you. But if you throw my daughter Mansa away you will know what you have never suspected.

MR TSI You are quarrelling about nothing. He is going to take her to Church.

NNA SU Do those who are taken to Churches go before the earnest money for their engagement is paid? I should like to know that.

MR TSI Why, they do not know the English way of doing things. We are only now getting civilized. Okadu's son is a scholar. Araba too is becoming a white lady. These two are now going to do things in the correct English style.

NNA SU Is this madman's tale true, or are you joking?

MR TSI It is true.

NNA SU If it is true, them I am going to my mother's house. I will never speak to you again. *(Exit)*.

MR TSI She will come back when she returns to her senses.

---

* Or, better spilt, perhaps?
  a [so] grossly slighted or b insulted. Literally, made or treated like a person of no account.

[70]

MRS BROF ⎫ *(Shaking hands)* Good-bye, Mr Tsiba. Good-bye
MR OK ⎭ Nna Sumpa. *(Exeunt R)*.

MR TSI *(To wife)* Akosua ab'rentsie n' ribewar Barbara: oribehyia n' ayifur.

NNA SU Oagyi n' yir a? Aben awawasem nyi i' e?

MR TSI Nyew. Oagyi n' yir.

NNA SUMPA Ogyi n' yir dabena na m'antzi 'i?

NNA SUMPA Ibiara mbebisà mi ba awar: ibiara mbotù ni tsir nsa. Se ema kwan ma woye mi ba sensanyi a onu ibohu m'enyimhar bi a owo m'hu *(preferable)*. Muwar wu 'i, m'ada w' fa m'ara abepim nde: m'inye wu du nten da. Na se etuw mi ba Mansa kyin dzi a, onu ibohu de biribi wo beebi.

MR TSI Iyi eriham gyan. Odzi n'ruko *Chapel*.

NNA SUMPA Nhon a wodzi hon kuko Tsapir 'i, wontutu hon tsir nsa a? Mibisa w'.

MR TSI Hhon wonnyim Aburekyir-amambu. Brana a hen enyiwa ribue yie a. Okadu ni ba n' oye skola. Araba su ridan Aburekyiraba. Nhon benu 'i na woribeye brofudzi n'mirkyimirkyi.

NNA SU Abodamfusem 'i ampa ana iridzi few?

MR TSI Ampa.

NNA SU Se ampa a, nna muruko mi na fie. Minnyinkasa w'anu bio *(Exit L)*.

MR TSI Ni tsir ba fie a, onu obesan aba.

MR TSI Woyè n' Aburekyir nsa-anu.

---

* Difficult to render the expression accurately in English. See p. 70.

SCENE THREE

Mr Onyimdzi's Smoking-room. Doors R & L.

Mr Onyimdzi seated smoking. A knock is heard.

MR ONY Yes!

Enter Mr Okadu.

MR OK You send for me, sir.

MR ONY Stand where I can see your face clearly.

MR OK *(Complying, but avoiding Mr Onyimdzi's eyes.)* Yes, sir.

MR ONY Now, sir, what is this I hear about Miss Tsiba? Who is responsible for the outrage?

MR OK I, sir.

MR ONY I am glad you have enough manhood left to admit that you are to blame. None the less, you have done the young lady a most flagrant wrong. What have you got to say for yourself?

MR OK Er——ummm——she came to—— to see Sister, and er—— she did not meet her.

MR ONY That is no reason why you should have behaved like a cad. Don't you see that you are placing the young lady in a distressing position? Then there is her mother. She thinks I am egging you on, and has come to my office more than twice. If I am to be held up for your pranks, you must do as I tell you, otherwise I shall give you the sack. Now, do you really mean to carry out that fool's scheme arranged by Mrs Brofusem, Mr Tsiba, and yourself?

MR OK Yes, sir. It is English style, sir. Mr Kwasia says it will

make no difference if we go to chapel soon. He too has gone
England.

MR ONY Kwasia be hanged! He was ordered to pay five shillings a week, I remember. He is an out and out scamp.

MR OK No, sir. He is a fine gentleman, sir.

MR ONY Like yourself, no doubt. Look here, I thought, a
moment ago, that there was some good in you, and I was
going to help you out of the mess. But you have shown yourself to me a most egregious ass. If you don't pay the damages
required by native custom, and afterwards make as much
amends as is possible, in such a case, by getting engaged to
her in the proper way, consider yourself dismissed from my
office. You have laid yourself open to a charge of seduction,
under the native law. I shall be surprised if you are not
formally charged before the *Oman*. I don't want any seducers
in my office. Clear out! *(Exit Mr Okadu R.)* It's just like that
numbskull to go to a fellow like Kwasia. Kwasia got into
trouble in England——a sickly affair with a servant: result,
open shame in court, and five shillings a week to pay.
A bally skivvy, if you please: not even a landlady's
daughter. *(A loud commotion is heard)* Hello, what's that?

*Door R. Bursts open, and in rushes Mr Okadu, wild-eyed, and
with collar and tie disarranged.*

MR OK I beg you, sir. Hide me somewhere. I met Miss Tsiba's
mother on the stairs, and she has nearly taken out my eyes.
She fell downstairs, so I run away.

MR ONY You fool, what have you done? Get in there.
(Opens door L. and thrusts in Mr Okadu)

*Door R. re-opens, and in rushes Nna Sumpa, struggling with
Half-crown.*

HALF Massa live here. He no want hambog.

[73]

NNA SU Say that to your mother Kroo Adwua. Get away. (…) Leave hold of my cloth.

MR ONY … What is it now, Nna Sumpa?

NNA SU You lying lawyer! Where is Okadu's son? With my own eyes, I saw him rush in here. When I get him, I shall tear him as I would rend a piece of cloth (…). If you do not hand… O, My Lord!

NNA SU Enyi wu na Kru Adwua. Fi nuhu! *(Pushes Half-crown away)* Gya mi tam m' *(Snatches cloth from Half-crown)*

MR ONY Half-crown, go away. Nna Sumpa, aben asem bio e?

NNA SU Ye, doya kohwinyi o! Okadu ni ba n' wo hin? Midzi m'ankasa m'enyiwa hun n' de oribehye ha. Mi nsa ka n' a, mibetsitsiw n' de mirisunsuan 'tam *(Quivering with rage, and breathlessly)* Se amfa n'——O, m'Ewuradzi! *(Raises her hands to her heart, and falls prone on the floor)*.

MR ONY Good Lord! *(Picks her up, and lays her on sofa)*

MR OK *(Entering L. very much frightened)* Oh, Mr Onyimdzi, I — am ——sor——ry.

MR ONY For goodness' sake, *don't* stand there gibbering. Run for a doctor. *(Exit Mr Okadu. R.)* What a thing to happen here. *(Places ear over woman's heart)* I wonder if she is really dead. I wish the doctor would come. Most awkward thing to happen here.

Enter R. Dr Ohweyie.

DR OHW Well, Onyimdzi, what's happened. A haggard fellow rushed in wildly, and said you wanted me immediatley.

MR ONY Glad you've come. Come and see. *(Draws doctor to sofa) Doctor carefully examines the woman, then slowly gets up, shaking his head.*

GR OHW Very sorry. Lady's dead. Heart failure, I think.

MR ONY What! Can't anything be done?

DR OHW Awfully sorry, old man, nothing whatever. It's Miss Tsiba's mother, isn't it?

MR ONY Yes. *(Walks up and down abstractedly)* Poor girl—first her good name, then her mother!

DR OHW Were you saying anything to me?

MR ONY No. Perhaps I was thinking aloud. I don't think I said anything.

[75]

DR OHW When you come to think of the difficulties I have passed through before I could have patients to operate on, you will get a headache. At first some said they were afraid, others said I couldn't do it, because only white men could operate, black surgeons being scarce. True, to a certain extent! When a white surgeon is unfortunate in an operation, nothing is said. If it had been a black man who had had such bad luck, the outcry would be loud and long. Now that I have operated successfully on so many people, the people call me "the Ripper"*. Kwesi!

KWESI Uncle ("Ankr" is the Fanti conception of "Uncle").

DR OHW Where is the dispenser?

KWESI He is dressing sores. He will soon finish.

DR OHW When he finishes tell him I want him (...) Look here (...) Let me see that hand. What did you do to it?

KWESI It swelled up, and I cut it with the knife in the operating room.

DR OHW What! Are you deaf? Haven't I told you never to take anything from the operating room? Dispenser!

DR OHW Why did you let Kwesi go into the operating room? Dispenser!

* In the mss. "The wielder of knives".

[ACT THREE]

SCENE ONE
Dr Ohweyie's Consultation-room.

Enter Doctor.

DR OHW Efuna a m'afuna ana nkyi mirinya nyimpa ma woaba
ma m'aye hon *operation* yi, se edwin hu a wu tsir bepaaw'.
Ahyesi n', wode wosuro. Ibinum su wosi de minkotum ye,
osiande Aburofu ara nku na wobotum *operation* ye, na ebibifu
dzi wonto ye. N'ara nyin'dzi: Burenyi ye *operation* na nyianu
n' wu a wonsi hwii; bibinyi a, nkye dede a wobeye a! Nkyi,
m'aye nyimpa pi ma hon apow m' aye hon dzin 'i, wofre m'
"Owoasikan". Kwesi!

Enter Kwesi, hands behind.

KWESI Ankr:
DR OHW *Dispenser* wo hin?
KWESI Orisee kur. Oka'akra ma oewie.
DR OHW Owie a, si n' de muruhwihwe n'. *(Kwesi turns round
to go. Doctor sees his hand bound)* Nhwe! *(Kwesi faces Doctor)*
Ma munhwe wu nsa 'i. Eye n' den? *(Undoing hand).*
KWESI Oahun, na midzi sikan n' a owo *operating-room* n' wo m'.
DR OHW E? *(Pulls his ear)* Woka w'asem a entsi, e? Minsi w'
de mma enfa biribiara wo *operating-room* ho bi a? Dispenser!

Enter dispenser.

DISP Yes, sir!
DR OHW Abenadzi 'ntsir na itsie Kwesi ma okuro *operating-
room* ho 'i?

[77]

DR OHW Did you shut the door?

DR OHW *(to Kwesi)* How did you manage to get the knife?

KWESI I went to sweep the room yesterday. When the dispenser left, I saw the knife lying there and I scratched the back of my hand with it.

DR OHW Don't do it again. If you repeat it I shall give you a sound whipping. Go!...

KWESI A man brought it.

DR OHW Tell him to wait.

DISP I did not see him, sir.

DR OHW Etu abuw n' m' a?

DISP I closed it myself after the operation yesterday.

DR OHW *(To Kwesi)* Eye den wunsa ka sikan n'?

KWESI Mikeprapra ho ndida, nna Dispenser fi ho a, muhun sikan n' de oda ho. Nna midzi twirow mi nsa ekyir.

DR OHW Ekur nyi n'. Eye adz'a otsi dem bio a, mubohwi w' ma ehu. Ko! *(Exit Kwesi. To Dispenser)*. See that nobody goes into the operating-room, except those who have a right to be there. *(Dispenser turns to leave)* And, Dispenser, did anyone come to worry an in-patient when I was out?

DISP *(Turning round)* A woman came to see her uncle's sister-in-law, but I sent her away.

DR OHW That's right. Never allow anybody to come in to see the patients unless he brings a permit. I have just asked the printers to print me some special cards for the purpose. We must be firm with the people: they do not understand these things. All right, dispenser! *(Exit Dispenser)* Only the other day, I nearly lost a patient, because sympathetic relations and friends kept visiting her from six a.m. to six p.m. and worrying her with talk.

Re-enter Kwesi with a letter.

KWESI Benyin bi dzi bee *(Handing letter)*.

DR OHW *(Taking it)* Si de ontwen. *(Exit Kwesi)*.

Doctor open letter, frowns, throws letter on table, gets up and walks up and down, once or twice stopping at the table and looking at the letter.

DR OHW Of all the dashed cheek. Listen. This blithering idiot writes: *(Reading)* "Dear Sir, — You attended my wife. My wife don't like me any more. People tell me she come to

KWESI Uncle!

DR OHW Tell the man who brought this letter to come here.

DR OHW Who sent you?

MAN Mr Wompem.

DR OHW Where does he live?

MAN He lives at Kotokuraba.

DR OHW Go and tell him that I do not understand his letter: and that if he is not looking for trouble, he should come here with his wife at once. You understand? Tell him that if he does not come I shall bring him before the King.

MAN I understand.

KWESI Uncle! (...) Uncle!

DR OHW What?

KWESI A school-girl wants to see you.

DR OHW Show her in.

[80]

your house. I beg you, doctor. I too fond of my wife. If you
send her away she will come. I beg you with God." Poor
devil! What delusion is it that's bothering him, I wonder?
And who told him that lie? I have attended many women.
I wonder who his wife is? Kwesi!

Re-enter Kwesi.

KWESI Ankr!

DR OHW Si benyin n' a odzi kratee 'i bee n' de ombra.

Exit Kwesi, Re-enter with Man. Exit Kwesi again.

MAN Morning, sir!

DR OHW Wana suma w'?

MAN Mr Wompem a.

DR OHW Otsi hin?

MAN Otsi Kotokuraba.

DR OHW Kesi ʀ' de ni kratee n' mintsi asi: na se ompe nuhu
asem a onu onyi ni yir n'mbra ha sisie ara. Atsi a? Sin de
oamba a, onu midzi n' boko Ahinfie.

MAN M'atsi *(Exit)*.

DR OHW Something has to be done with these idiots. Because
they themselves can't be trusted with women, they think
everybody else is like them. I have examined no women
patients except in the presence of their female relations or
their husbands. Which of these bally women is it?

Re-enter Kwesi.

KWESI Ankr! *(Doctor, pacing abstractedly up and down does not
hear)* Ankr! *(Goes after Doctor Ankr! Pulls doctor's coat)*.

DR OHW E? *(Turns round)*.

KWESI Skur-*girl* bi rihwihwe w'.

DR OHW Ma ombra. *(Exit Kwesi)*.

GIRL I have come for some medicine: I have not been feeling well since school was over.

DR OHW What is the matter?

GIRL The thing, whatever it is, is in my side! it gives me a sharp pain.

DR OHW (...) Let me hear you breathe.

GIRL It has now sunk into my stomach. Oh! I am dying!

DR OHW What?

GIRL It is going further down.

DR OHW I see! Listen. If you want me to examine you, go and come with your mother. Do you take me for a child? What is it you want?

DR OHW (...) Don't cry. Who sent you here?

GIRL I came here straight from school.

DR OHW Don't tell lies. School closes at four. (...) It is half-past five. When did you visit after school?

GIRL I went to see Mr Seehon.

DR OHW So, *he* sent you here?

GIRL Yes, sir.

DR OHW Very good. Go. Try to be good.

Enter School-girl, with books in her hand, walking very bashfully.

GIRL Good afternoon, Doctor!

DR OHW You mean good evening, I suppose, Good evening!
Please, sit.

GIRL Mipun skur na min*feel* yie, nna m'aba de ma m'edur.

DR OHW Abenadzi ye w'

GIRL Adzi n' ohye mi mfi m': okaw m' dwii.

DR OHW *(Applying stethoscope)* Gyi ahum ma mintsie.

GIRL Adzi kur n' Oabehye mi yefun m'. A! Muruwu! *(Doubles up)*.

DR OHW *(Surprised)* E?

GIRL Ekyi orisan.

DR OHW O! Nhwe, se erihwihwe ma m'ahwe adzi kur n' a,
onu ko na enyi wu na mbra. Edwin de afraba nyi m' a?
Abenadzi na erihwihwe?

GIRL Er——er——*(Bursts into tears)*.

DR OHW Now, now. Mna 'nsu. Wana si w' de bra?

GIRL Mifi skur ara na mibee.

DR OHW Mma indzi akohwisem. Wopun skur ndon 'nan.
(Looks at his watch) Woabo ndon 'num mpem'. Ifi skur n'
ekuro wana nkyen?

GIRL Mikuro *Papa* Seehon ni nkyen.

DR OHW O! Onu si w' de bra a?

GIRL Nyew.

DR OHW Oye, ko! Bo mbodzin ye adz 'a oye. *(Exit Girl, very
much abashed)*. By Jove! Here's another. First, one man
thinks I am keeping his wife: then an old rogue sends me a
girl, when he is tired of her, thinking I shall behave to her as
he did. Really, it is most difficult to practise here, and be
happy at the same time.

[83]

KWESI Mr Tsiba is here.
DR OHW Show him in.

MR TSI (...) Oh! How sad is the parent's lot!

Re-enter Kwesi.

KWESI Papa Tsiba aba ha.

DR OHW Enyi n' mbra.

Re-enter Kwesi followed by Mr and Miss Tsiba. Exit Kwesi.

DR OHW Good evening, Mr Tsiba! Good evening Miss Tsiba! Please, sit. Now, what can I do for you?

MR TSI I bring my girl: she is sick: feel her.

DR OHW *(Aside)* By Jove: she is in trouble: I can see that. *(To Miss Tsiba)* You are not well?

MISS TSI Yes, doctor. Mrs Brofusem says it is koo koo. It is in my stomach.

DR OHW I see. Permit me. *(Examines her slowly. Takes Mr Tsiba aside, and whispers to him).*

MR TSI *(Wildly)* Impossible! It can't happen! My girl is virginity. *(Turns round, and sees Girl weeping).*

DR OHW There is no doubt about it.

MR TSI Hello, Barbara, Why you cry? Doctor say you get baby. You are not well: all the concerts and picnics and balls make you tired. Speak what's matter with you.

MISS TSI Kookoo.

DR OHW *(To Mr Tsiba)* If you doubt my word, take her to the colonial hospital. You will find a white doctor there. Perhaps you will be satisfied with his diagnosis. I should add that the thing is four months old.

MISS TSI Only three mo——*(Stops as unexpectedly as she began, and bursts afresh into tears).*

MR TSI Eh? What you say? What is three months?

DR OHW There you are: she has confessed.

MR TSI I am sadness: I am grief: Doctor, she is to be taken to Chapel soon. O! Awu ye yew duduw: She can't go like that: it will pour uncleanness on the church. O, do not tell anybody.

DR OHW A professional man has to be silent regarding several things that he finds out in the course of his practice.

MR TSI I never hear that. But, doctor, you make plenty operation, make her operation, and take it out.

DR OHW It can't be done. Don't you know it's criminal?

MR TSI *(Falling on his knees, and embracing Doctor's knees)* I beg you with God. For Christ's sake, doctor, make her operation.

DR OHW You are evidently confusing me with God. Please don't pray to me as you do in your religious moments, or you will make me laugh. Only God can do what you want me to do without coming into conflict with the authorities, and I am sure even he cannot do so before the proper time. *I* am quite human, I assure you, and have such human limitation as compel me to consider my reputation and practice.

MR TSI I have many cocoa land. I will pay fifty pounds.

DR OHW Look here, Mr Tsiba, understand that I am a doctor ——a member of an honourable profession——not a quack. I am pledged to save as many lives as I can, even at the risk of my own. You come here and ask me to destroy one life, and place another life in danger. Do you take me for a scoundrel?

MR TSI She is to be taken to chapel. Do the operation, and I will pay one hundred pounds.

DR OHW I don't wish to be hard on you, but I feel this moment very much like giving you a good kick. What do you mean by coming into my consulting-room to offer me insults?

MR TSI I do not offer insult; I offer money. Do it, and I will pay two hundred pounds.

DR OHW Go! Go! before you force me to throw you out of this room. Miss Tsiba, if I may advise you, leave Nature to do her work: you will only destroy yourself, or else lay by trouble for yourself in the future, if you attempt to interfere with the natural course of things. Please, go!

MR TSI (...) How sad is the parent's lot. (...) Let us go. I have
wasted a lot of money on you. You have brought disgrace
upon me.

KWESI A man and his wife want to see you.
DR OHW Tell them to come.

DR OHW What is it you say I have to do with you?
MR W'S WF I have said nothing, sir.
DR OHW Ask your husband to tell you what it is. He wrote me
that because of me you care no more for him.
MR W'S WF (...) Did you write such a letter?
MR WO Yes.
MR W'S WF Have you no sense of shame? Do you want to get
into trouble? I was suffering from a boil, and Doctor lanced it:
so I sent him a little present of mangoes and melons.
MR WO Why didn't you tell me about it?
MR W'S WF I did not buy them with your money.
DR OHW If you want to quarrel, go home and quarrel. What I
want to tell you is this: if anyone says I am fooling with his
wife I shall take it that he wants to blackmail me, because
if it was true, he would prosecute me for it. I shall hand over

MR TSI Doctor, I beg! I beg! Have mercy! I will pay two
hundred and fifty pounds. It is too much money: but I
have many cocoa——

DR OHW If you do not go, I shall be forced to send for police.
Kwesi!

MR TSI Doctor, I beg. Don't call police. I go. I go. Awu ye
yew! *(To Miss Tsiba)* Besin ma yenko. M'abo wu hu kaw
gyan. Egu m'enyim asi. *(Exeunt Mr and Miss Tsiba).*

DR OHW Good riddance! *(Picks up the letter of the table)* I wonder
when this other fool is coming with his wife? *(Enter Kwesi)*
Yes?

KWESI Benyin bi na ni yir aba ha.

DR OHW Si hon de wombra. *(Exit Kwesi).*

Enter Mr Wompem and his wife.

MR WO You send for me, sir, and we have come.

DR OHW Is that your wife?

MR WO Yes, sir.

DR OHW Ewu na esi miriye w' den? *(To Mr Wompem's wife).*

MR W'S WF Muwura, m'inka hwi.

DR OHW Bisa wu kun ma onka asem kur n' nkyire w'. Okyirew
m' de emi 'ntsir impe n' bio.

MR W'S WF *(To Mr Wompem)* Ewu kyirew dem kratee yi a?

MR WO Nyew.

MR W'S WF Adzi nye w' enyitu e? Aben amandzinyasem na
iridzi 'i? Pompo bo m', nna datsir bo m' ma m': nna mibe-
kye n' adzi kakra: mango na anemuna.

MR WO Abenadzi ntsir na anka ankyire m'?

MR W'S WF Mindzi wu sika kotoi.

DR OHW Se woribeham a, onu wonko fie nkeham. Dz'a mir-
ihwihwe m'aka akyire hon nyi de: ibiara si de mirigur ni
yir hu a, onu mibesi de orihwihwe *oablackmail* m', osiande
se ampa a, nkye n'ara bekesaman m'. Midzi dem nyimpa n'

any such person to a lawyer. Do you think I went to England,
suffered so much, bore a great deal of cold, and paid so much
money, all in order to fool with other peoples' wives?

MR W's WF Doctor, forgive.

DR OHW Go away.

MR W's WF You will hear more of this.

bema *lawyer*. Wodwin de mukuro Aburekyir kofuna pi, mikosow awow, na mitua sika pi, ama m'anya kwan agugur ndihyi nyirnum hu a?

MR WO I beg you, sir. *(Kneeling)*.

MR W'S WF Datsir, ma onka. *(Kneeling)*.

DR OHW Womfi ha nko!

MR W'S WF *(To husband)* Impire ebetsi po!

SCENE TWO

A Meeting of the "Cosmopolitan Club".

President, Vice-President, Secretary and Treasurer seated at a table, L. member reading paper standing at desk C. on which are placed a cooler and a tumbler. Members seated, R.

READER *(Drinking some water, and reading)* "In conclusion of this treatise on "How to be a Gentleman", I must embrace opportunity to impress force on you to say that without tailors and hatters and shoemakers, gentlemen, we are nothing."

1ST MEM Well said!

2ND MEM Praise God!

3RD MEM A Daniel come to judgement!

VICE-PR Amen!

PRES *(Gavelling sharply)* Order! Silence in court! Continue, brother.

READ *(Bowing to president, then to members)* I must express to you my thanks and gratitude, gentlemen, for your most vociferous ovation. *(Reading)* "To continue my dissertation,

[91]

I say, without tailors and hatters and shoemakers, we will be savages."

1ST MEM God forbid!

2ND MEM Heaven forfend!

3RD MEM *Deo* not being *volente!*

VICE PR Amen!

PRES *(Suddenly waking from dozing, clapping, and as suddenly gavelling)* Shut up! *(To reader)* Mr Oehumuwa, go on, and don't mind them.

READ "Without these people, we sill walk barefoot. We will wear native dress. Our feet and arms would be naked, and indecent. But with the help of these useful workmen we have mentioned, and, I must add, with the help of European merchants, who have given us ham and bacon and milk and sugar and——"

1ST MEM Marmalade.

READ "——and marmalade and jam and lemonade and beer and stout and champagne——ripe, mellifluous, elevating champagne, and——"

2ND MEM Good old fizz!

READ "——brandy and whiskey——"

TREAS And soda.

READ "——and gin and rum."

3RD MEM And vermouth.

READ "Without Europeans we have only palm-wine to drink, which only bushmen drink. No scholar who wants to be a gentleman must drink palm-wine. It is better to be placed in a state of obliviousness of surroundings and circumstances and environments by European drinks than by palm-wine: it is more gentlemanly. In August, when it is too cold, there is nothing like whiskey or vermouth to keep you warm. And on Sundays, before going to Chapel, or Church, which is more fashionable, it is good to take a little gin and bitters

[92]

as an appetiser, in order to relish the sermon. One word more: to be a gentleman, we must imitate Europeans". *(Sits amid loud cheers)*.

1ST MEM You ought to be a lawyer.

2ND MEM Or an auctioneer.

VICE PRES Or a minister of the gospel.

PRES *(Gavelling loudly)* Silence! Order! Gentlemen, we must congratulate and felicitate with Mr Oehumuwa, the honourable reader of the paper, on his wonderful achievement. The debate is now exposed to the meeting.

1ST MEM I agree with him.

2ND MEM I think the treatise is very nice. There are many big words in it. I have made notes in my note-book, and I will learn them by heart, and use them when I speak. I thank the honourable reader of the treatise.

3RD MEM Mr Oehumuwa's treatise is comprehensible: he has said all I was going to say.

4TH MEM Same here.

5TH MEM I also.

MR OKADU I have something more to add. The eminent estimable and learned reader of the treatise, has not said the most important saying. Without Europeans, there would be no churches, and without churches, we could not be married: there would be no weddings. Without weddings we will not get the chance to speechify in public. Last, but by no means least, without Europeans, there will be no lorries, and only lorry-weddings are grand.

1ST MEM Well said!

2ND MEM Logical!

PRES *(Gavelling loudly)* Order! I thank Mr Okadu for his invaluable addition to the debate. The debate is now terminated. The proximate debate will take place in six months' time. We have to make a concert, then picnic, with lorry, then we will have athletic sports. We will give "At Home" next week, then grand ball, then evening-party, then conversazione, and a garden-party. The white men will come: so we have no time for debates. We must prepare well for them. The Librarian has ordered two dozen copies of " *don't*", and three dozen copies of "*how to dance*". When we have learned all by heart, we will make further additions to our bibliotheca. The Secretary will now read an invitation we have received.

SEC Ahem! "Mr Aldiborontiphoscophornio Chrononhontonthologos Tsiba politely requests the pleasure of the company of the officers and Members of the "Cosmopolitan Club' at Hallelujah Church, on Thursday, the 1st prox. to witness the nuptial ceremony between his daughter, Barbara Ermyntrude, and Mr Alexander Archibald Octavius Okadu, at 2.30 p.m. and thence to Hamilton House for refreshments. R.S.V.P. to Mr Owombi."

PRES Is the invitation to be accepted? *(Members all hold up their hands)* Carried. We have been asked to manage the jollification and refreshments at Hamilton House, which will be of Lucullian magnificence. I will be Master of Ceremonies, the Secretary will propose the Bride and Bridegroom, the Treasurer will propose the Bridesmaids. The Vice-President will propose the parents of the Bride and Bridegroom. Lastly, at the last Committee-meeting, it was decided to add two new rules to our regulations. (1) "No member must greet people in native dress." (2) "No member must talk the native language in the day-time." Has anyone any objections to make?

Members confer awhile.

1ST MEM I beg to——
2ND MEM *(Pulling 1st member's coat)* Wait!

[94]

1st member sits. Gets up again after a few minutes.

IST MEM I beg to propose amendment. Many of us get mothers
and female relatives, who do not speak English, also wear
native dress. I and my fellow——

PRES Wait! (*1st member sits, while officers confer*) We think it
does not matter: for the first of the new rules, we will allow
deserving exceptions: for the second, you can always trans-
late what you say.

IST MEM I beg to propose that all the motions must be carried.

2ND MEM I beg to second the motion.

PRES Please, vote. (*Members show hands*) Carried unanimously.
The meeting is over.

Sudden rush for door by all.

SCENE THREE

A Wedding Reception at Hamilton House.

*Confusion and fine clothing. Table laden with drinkables, glasses,
plates of cut cake, buns, and the wedding-cake. R. chairs arranged R
half of stage, benches L. crush of female* efuratamfu *and children.
L. enter, L. members of "Cosmopolitan Club". In frock coats,
carrying their silk hats shouting themselves hoarse in the attempt to
introduce order, and elbowing a way through the crush.*

MEM'S "C C" Room! Room! Bride and Bridegroom are coming!

*Crowd fall on benches, right and left. Enter, L. Miss Tsiba and
Mr Okadu dressed as bride and bridegroom, Mr Tsiba's boy as
page, holding up Miss Tsiba's train, two girls as bridesmaids.*

Mr Tsiba, in frock coat, holding silk hat, a young man as best man, Mr and Mrs Brofusem, male and female ahyentarfu. *Old and young, filling the chairs. Two young ladies go round with cakes, two young men with glasses. Two female* efuratamfu *go, L, with calabashes of buns: Pandemonium, L, among the children. President of "Cosmopolitan Club" makes two expeditions to table, returning with a plate of cake, glasses, a bottle of whiskey and a bottle of soda to part where members of "Cosmopolitan Club" are sitting together. They share. Babel of voices. Bride statuesque. Bridegroom semi-rigid. Mr Tsiba all smiles and very excitable. Mrs Brofusem, looking round through lorgnette, highly gratified. Mr Brofusem profoundly bored.*

1ST MEM "C C" Ah! Cake is nice: all due to white man.

2ND MEM Of course. Ha! Ha! Let us be glad we are modern born.

3RD MEM Whiskey is good: it warms your inside. He! He!

ALL *(Drinking)* Chin-chin! Ho! Ho! Ho!

MRS BROF *(Going up to Mr Tsiba)* The bride must cut the cake, you know.

MR TSI *(Jumping up exitedly)* Er——where is President? Ah, there he is. *(Goes to President "C.C".)* Come and begin.

PRES "C C" *(Going to table, and rapping loudly)* Silence! Silence there! Order! *Order!* *(Shouting)* The bride will now cut the wedding-cake.

Mrs Brofusem jumps up and whispers to Miss Tsiba. Then Mr Okadu and Miss Tsiba walk arm in arm to table.

MRS BROF *(To Mr Okadu)* Take the knife and stick the cake. *(Mr Okadu obeys)* Good. *(To Miss Tsiba)* Hold the knife and cut it to the plate. *(Miss Tsiba cuts the cake in great confusion)*.

Loud applause.

MR TSI She has done it! Hear! Hear! She has done it!

MEM's "C C" Champagne! Champagne!

Glasses of champagne are handed round.

PRES "C C" Ahem! The next item on the programme is the health of the bride and bridegroom, which Mr Kyirewfu will propose.

Cheers.

MR KYI *(Shouting above the din)* I have great pleasure for proposing the health of the bride and bridegroom today. The manifestations of incredible merrimentations has displayed in this capacious hall due to wedding matrimonial jollification. Long live the bride and bridegroom!

Loud applause. Mr Kyirewfu sits, wiping his face.

MR KYI *(To neighbour)* What did I say? Did I speak well?

NEIGH Very nice: almost like a European.

PRES "C C" Ahem! The next item on the programme is: the bridegroom will respond to previous health.

Cheers.

MR OK On behalf affectionate consort and self, I thank you all for coming to see my wedding. I thank you all for wishing long life. Our matrimonial and connubial amiability assuring our nuptial knot is inextricably woven with the minister of God Almighty.

Cheers.

PRES "C C" Ladies and gentlemen, silence for the next item on the programme: Mr Nkuntee will propose the health of the bridemaids.

MR NKU My eyes are effusive of their joyful lachrimosity to

perceive *coram* us this reception, and its bride and bridesmaids of amazing pulchritudity. I harbour expectation that they too will be espoused, and not recommend celibacy to young men, and will be led to the hymeneal altar.

Cheers.

PRES "C C" Order! The best-man will respond.

BEST It is only a fortnight ago that I officiated in the same capacity as best man at a reception, that of my *fidus Achates* Mr Dwasufew. I thank the gentleman who proposed the bridesmaids. I am sure they too will be conducted to the hymeneal altar with considerable *eclat*, and people will not be wanting to chant their epithalamium with becoming vociferosity.

Uproarious applause.

1ST MEM "C C" Fine speechification (*To 2nd member* "C.C.")

2ND MEM Like a European.

MR KYI (*Jealously*) I don't think much of it: he read from memory.

PRES "C C" Order! Silence! Mr Odziekyir will now propose the health of the parents of the bride and bridegroom.

MR ODZ At these magnificent celebration of happiness consequent on inosculation of *viniculum matrimonii* affords me utmost satisfaction to propose the health of the parents of the bride and bridegroom.

Cheers.

PRES "C C" The next item on the programme is: Mr Tsiba will respond to preceding health.

MR TSI (*In great trepidation*) Er——gentlemen——er——and ladies, I——er——I thank——you, sir——no, ma'am. Er——I am glad. Praise touch God for the kindness he has taken to show me.

GR AK Because all who are at this gathering are Fantis, I will
speak in Fanti. It is only when the advice I am about to give
is given in Fanti that anyone is likely to profit by any valuable
counsel it may contain. What I have to say to the bride and
her husband is that those of our fathers, who, for religious
reasons, took their wives into Churches to be married, lived
happily as man and wife according to native tradition: the
little of European life discoverable in the lives of our fathers
was due to their change of faith. If you, too, wish to lead a
happy married life, be not swayed by outward appearances
to conduct your wives in to churches, otherwise your married
lives will be miserable. I trust the young man and young
woman before us went into the church this afternoon with
pure aspirations. May their life be prosperous.

ACT THREE

Amen! I am glad that my daughter has marriage English
fashion.

Cheers.

PRES "C C" Now we will call on Mr Oehubi, one of our young
men who have taken ladies to the hymeneal altar, to address
us
MR OEH I think the best happiness from marriage life is result
of kissing. I advice the couple to learn how to kiss. I recommend the new wife to always meet her husband when he is
coming from business, and kiss him on the door-step. That
is the way to be happy though married. I read it in a book
that it is done in England; and since I tried it, I have had no
more trouble with my wife.

Loud applause.

PRES "C C" Now Grandfather Akodee will advise the bride and
bridegroom.
GR AK Onam de nhon a wowo ha nyina woye Mfantsifumba n'
'ntsir n', *(Cries of "no Fanti, please", "this is European affair")*
mirikasa Mfantsi, Mfantsina se wokasa n'wo ha a, afutu a
mirubotu n' wo ha 'i, se mfasu bi wo m'a, ibinum befa. Dz'a
muwo ka kyire ayifur na ni kun nyi de: Hen egyanum a, asor
'ntsir, wodzi hon yirnum kuro Asor-awar mu n', wodzi hon
ebibidwin na hon tsitsiamambu na wodzi warii ma wohun
anu. Brofudzi kakraebi na owo ewuako-mpenyinfu n' hon
abrabo m': na onu su po ofir Asor. Se nhon su worihwihwe
abo bra ma woehu anu a, mma wontsin beguadu-few du
mfa hon nyirnum nko Asordan m'. *(Members of "Cosmopolitan Club" shake hands with Miss Tsiba and Mr Okadu and
exeunt, L. scowling)* Woye dem a, hon awar nkoso. Muwo
ehyidadu de abrentsie na akataesia a hen enyi tua hon yi

[101]

NANA KAT Where is Tsiba? They say he is here. Get out of my way. Where is Tsiba? Now, Tsiba, do you wish me to un- ...derstand that you are here merry-making.

IST TAM There he is.

NANA KAT Where is he?

IST TAM There he is, sitting by Mrs Brofusem.

NANA KAT (...) O man of ill omen. What are you doing here? Give me back my daughter. Where is Sumpa? Have you not killed her with your heartlessness? And where is Araba? Do you want to kill her, too? That I will prevent.

NANA KAT Go away, you accursed people. (...) Tsiba, I am surprised at you. Have you, whose wife died a week ago, left the room of the widower's confinement to attend a wedding? They say Araba Mansa, too, is here. Where is she?

NANA KAT (...) Araba, child of my beloved child. (...) Araba, are you now an orphan? (...) O, how bitter is Life! Sumpa, my daughter, my beautiful tender-hearted, my humble-souled daughter, that you should be thus served! Your husband has neglected your obsequies, and your daughter had not observed your funeral custom.

wodzi adwin a otsiw kor Asordan m' ewiabir 'i. Mima hon
awarso!

*Enter, L, Nana Katawirwa, followed by two female atamfurafu,
in a fury.*

NANA KAT Tsiba wo hin? Wosi owo ha. Womfi mi kwan m'.
Tsiba wo hin? Nhwe, Tsiba o, ewu wo ha risepew wu hu a?
1ST TAM Onu nyi n'.
NANA KAT Owo hin?
1ST TAM Ona na oku Ewuraba Mrs Brofusem ni nkyen n'.
NANA KAT *(Rushing at Mr Tsiba)* Ye, busuanyi o! Eriye den wo
ha? Mirigyi mi ba. Sumpa wo hin? Enkyi edzi w'etsimodzin
eku n'? Araba su wo hin? Erihwihwe eku nu su a? Onu dzi
minnyintsie w'.

*Mr Tsiba, seeing Nana Katawirwa's rush, moves wildly backwards,
falling on Mrs Brofusem, who shrieks. Mr Brofusem and the best
man, to the rescue, attempt to pull Nana Katawirwa away, but are
attacked by the two atamfurafu.*

NANA KAT Womfi mu du, ebusuafu. *(To Mr Tsiba, with arms
Akimbo)* Ho! Ho! Hoo——o! Tsiba, mubo w'etsifi, Ndenda'
wotwi wu yir wu a, efi ekunadan m'aboku ayifurasi? Wosi
Araba mansa su wo ha. O-wo hin?

*Mrs Brofusem tries to draw veil over Miss Tsiba's face. Nana
Katawihwa sees and intercepts Mrs Brofusem, peering into Miss
Tsiba's face.*

NANA KAT Araba, mi doba ni ba! *(Kneels, embraces Miss Tsiba's
waist, and starts weeping)* Awu! Araba, aye egya'nka ba?
(Rises wringing her hands) Epe! Iwiadzi ye yew ai! Mi ba
Sumpa, eba feefe, eba a otsi ma nyimpa, eba birefu, dz'a
ehu nyi'i? Wu kun anye w'eyi, wu ba su anye w'eyi.

2ND TAM (...) Grandmother, let us go: day is closing. You rushed here as soon as you arrived; you dit not sit down to rest.

NANA KAT (...) Amba, leave me to think. It is a bitter world! It is a bitter world! (...) As soon as I received your letter, I set out, when I arrived, I was told that both you and Araba were here. What are you doing here? (...) What does this white dress you are wearing mean? What are all these people here for?

MISS TSI (...) I——am——a——bride.

NANA KAT Say that again.

NANA KAT (...) Take care how you court trouble; this child is nothing to you.

MR TSI She is Okadu's bride. We have only just come out of the church. This is the reception. We did it in the English manner.

NANA KAT It seems to me these wines on the table have made you all drunk. I know that nobody has asked my grand-daughter in marriage. Don't tell me any barbarous tales. A wedding should be celebrated in the night. I have never seen a daylight wedding except among churchgoers, who, alone, do such strange things; I did not know that you were a church-goer.

MR TSI I say we did it in the English manner.

NANA KAT If this is English, then the English are barbarians. (...) I am your mother's mother: you belong to my family. Come away with me.

Miss Tsiba bursts into tears, and all the women at the reception start weeping.

2ND TAM *(Drying her eyes)* Nana, mayenko: adzi risa! ifi kwan nam a idu fie, anku daadzi na edzi enguan ba ha 'i.

NANA KAT *(Gently pushing woman aside)* Amba, ma mundwin. Iwiadzi ye yew ai! *(Breaks out afresh into tears)* Iwiadzi ye yew! Iwiadzi ye yew! *(To Mr Tsiba, calmly)* Mi nsa ka wu kratee n' ara na misi m'. Muduri na wosi m' de ewo ha, na Araba su wo ha. Woriye den wo ha? *(To Miss Tsiba)* Atar fufuw 'i a ehye 'i su e? Nyimpa pi yi woriye den wo ha?

MISS TSI *(Sobbing)* Mi——y—ye——a——yi——fur.

NANA KAT Ka bio ma m'intsie.

MR OK *(Placing an arm round Miss Tsiba)* She says she is bride. She is my wife.

NANA KAT *(Angrily removing Mr Okadu's hand)* Hwe yie ma inya amandzi: eba 'i ye wu hwi bi a.

MR TSI Okadu ni yir a. Siesieara yefi Asordan m' ba ha. Yeye n' Brofu nsa'nu. Ayifur-pun asi nyi 'i.

NANA KAT Oye m' de nsa a osisi pun 'i du 'i ama woabubuw. Mi nyim de mi nana 'i ibiara mbebisa n' awar. Mma mbedzi amansinasem nkyire m'. Ayifur su wohyia n'anufua. Munhun ewiabirayifur-hyia da. Asormba na woye dem ananadzi: minnyim de wu su ko Asor.

MR TSI Mide ye ye n' Abrofu nsa'nu.

NANA KAT Se Brofudzi nyi 'i a, nna Abrofu ye amansinafu. *(To Miss Tsiba)* Wu na ni na nyi m': m'ebusua na ebo. Besin ma yenko. *(Takes Miss Tsiba's hand, and turns to leave the hall).*

NANA KAT Learn to respect the mother who bore you. (i.e. if you would be rude, be rude to your own mother.)

2ND FISH (...) Here, Kwesi, is your mother at home?

1ST BOY Yes. (...) I have won two!

1ST FISH (...) Good afternoon, Mr Abireku! (...) I beg your pardon.

OLD FISH I thank you. Look out!

Mr Okadu attempts to force Nana Katawir's hand away. Nana Katawirwa slaps him in the face.

NANA KAT Ma w'enyi nso wu na a owu w'.

Exeunt Nana Katawirwa, Miss Tsiba and the two atamfurafu attending on Nana Katawirwa. Enter members of "Cosmopolitan Club", and surround Mr Okadu.

MEM'S "C C" Don't mind this savage woman. They say she has always lived in far off hinterland. She does not understand: she will soon be all right.

SCENE FOUR

A street outside Nana Katawirwa's house.

An old fisherman, seated L. front of stage, making nkow *out of palm-leaves, some boys, seated R back corner of stage playing* nte (?). *Two young women, seated R. front corner of stage playing* ewar. *Door of Nana Katawirwa's house, L. enter, L. A young fisherman in wet loin-cloth, carrying net, paddle and* birefi, *smoking short clay pipe. Enter, R. another young fisherman, in full native dress, face chalked unmistakably. Furry cap pulled over his ears, smoking cigarette.*

2ND FISH *(Walking towards. L. to 1st boy)* Hei, Kwesi! wu na wo fie a?

1ST BOY Nyew *(Stretching hands over* Kete*)* Ebien! Ebien!

1ST FISH *(Walking towards R)* Egya Abireku, mi ma w' aha!
(Collides with second fisherman) Kuse!

OLD FISH Ye abraw! Hwe kwan m'.

2ND FISH I beg your pardon.

1ST FISH (...) Hello, Kwodwo, where are you going? Did you
not go out to sea today?

2ND FISH Why. Do you not realize that I have signed a
contract? I work now for the Boating Association I went to
the white man to get an advance. I am on my way to my
wife's house.

1ST FISH You lucky fellow. I went out to sea early this morning,
but have taken very little fish. I go to get some *dokun* to eat.
I am hungry.

2ND FISH Good evening Mr Abireku. Do you still make your
own twine, when there is so much European twine in the
stores?

OLD FISH I thank you! Who will make it for me if I do not
make it myself? European twine does not last.

2ND FISH You are old; you should not work so much.

OLD FISH Yes, I have lived long. If only my son, Kwamina, had
not ruined himself with drink, perhaps he would now be
working to support me. Rum has a good deal to account for!

BOYS I have won two! Another!

1ST Y W Shall we now play *enamnam* or *mbapa?*

2ND Y W Let is play *mbapa*.

1ST Y W Adwua, look!

FASH TAM Morning, white man!

2ND FISH Kuse!

1ST FISH *(To 2nd fisherman)* Na iyi e? Kwodwo, eriko hin?
Nde anko pu m' a?

2ND FISH Huo! Innyim de nde m'akasain kontragyi bi a?
Nde miye *Botu* Association edwuma. Mukuro burenyi ho
kegyi adabans. Muruko mi yir fie nyi.

1ST FISH A! Wu kra m' wo adzi ai! Anapa etu na mukuro
pu m'. Minnya nam biara. Muruko m'akohwihwe dokun bi
m'edzi: ekom dzi m'. *(Exit. R)*.

2ND FISH Egya Abireku, kudibin. Brofu-huma pi yi a woton
n' fiadzi 'i, ewu edahu ara ye w'ahuma?

OLD FISH Y'aye! Se m'anyea, wana beye ama m'? Brofuhuma
nkyer suw.

2ND FISH Aye akodee: onnyi de eye edwuma pi. *(Exit, L)*.

OLD FISH Ehee! Miba wiadzi akyer. Se miba Kwamina amfa
nsanum ansee nu hu a, nkye ibir'i onu na oye edwuma hwe
m'. Muna-nsa a, oaye bi!

BOYS Ebien! Ebien! Oapei!

1ST Y W Nkyi su yentuw enamnam ana mbapa?

2BD Y W Ma yentuw mbapa.

Young women begin to re-arrange the ambadwiwa. *Enter, L, a
female* tamfura-nyi *in elaborate costume, face white with chalk,
holding up a parasol, and carrying a hand-bag. Enter white man,
R. in shirt-sleeves, white trousers and shoes, helmet, smoking
cigarette.*

1ST Y W *(Making a mouth at Fashionable Tamfuranyi)* Adwua,
nhwe!

WH MAN *(Stopping to chat with Fashionable Tamfuranyi)* Hello,
Esi!

FAS TAM Burenyi, mon!

[109]

FASH TAM Do you suppose one has to dress only for picnics? I went out. I am going home.

FASH TAM Very good.

1ST Y W Wonders never cease. "Cloth ladies" now-a-days sew their cloth like the skirts of "Frock ladies". They wear petticoats, chemises, stockings and shoes!

2ND Y W Just look at her parasol and her hand-bag!

OLD FISH The world has gone wrong! These are they who sell our country to white men. Some people, when they are hard up, give their daughters in marriage to white men—all for the sake of money. Years ago, only slaves were given in marriage to white men. The world has gone wrong! Just fancy that she has so much finery on her person in these Kaiser-days, when there is little food to buy.

1ST BOY (...) Is your marble pressed? It wins many marbles.

2ND Y W Now we are quits.

MR TSI May I enter?

MR TSI (...) May I come in?

POLICE (in pidgin English) Keep out of this! We are going for the woman who lives in there.

MR TSI Look here, Okadu, what do you want here?

WH MAN Morning! What's the game? Picnic or wedding?

FASH TAM Wosi *picnic* ara nku na *wodress* ko a? Mupuei. Muruko fie.

WH MAN *(Shaking hands, and whispering)* See you later. *(Exit. L)*.

FASH TAM Oye! *(Exit, R)*.

IST Y W Dz'a oriba, oye hu! Nde *efuratamfu* su wopam hon tam de *ahyentarfu* hon asitar. Wohye petkot na hyift na asitagyir na asupatsir su.

2ND Y W Nhwe ni kyim! Nhwe ni kotoku!

OLD FISH Iwiadzi ase! Iyinum na woton hen kurow ma Aburofu 'i. Mpenyin fu binum se hon hu ka a, nna wodzi hon mba amima Abrofu awar Sika ara 'ntsir. Nkaanu n' ekwan m'-fu na wodzi hon mima Abrofu awar. Iwiadzi ase! W'ara Kaiza-bir yi a nyimpa nnya edziban po nto 'i, onu oenya ndzemba a otsitsi dem ahyihye nu hu.

IST BOY *(To another)* Wu nte 'i buhyiw a? Obo nte papa.

2ND Y W Nkyi m'etua mi kaw. *(Stretches herself)*.

Enter Mr Tsiba, R, wiping his face, and fanning himself with his helmet, under an Umbrella.

MR TSI Ah! Too hot! Too hot! I sweat too much! *(Goes to door, L, and knocks)* Ago——o!

Enter Mr Okadu, R, wiping his face and fanning himself with his handkerchief, followed by a policeman in a cape, also wiping his face. Mr Okadu walks to door, L.

MR OK *(To policeman)* Come! This is the house. *(Tries to open door)*.

MR TSI *(To Mr Okadu)* Stop!

POLICE *(To Mr Tsiba)* W'a's matta you no lef am? We wan' get woman live here.

MR TSI Nhwe, Okadu, erihwihwe abenadzi wo ha?

MR TSI (...) You are insolent.

OLD FISH Calm yourself, Mr Tsiba. You know that young men of these days have no respect for their elders.

OLD FISH (...) Strike me, if you want to. Is this your education? Is this your enlightenment? Because you wear European clothes, can you not distinguish those who are old enough to be grandfathers to you.

1ST Y W Mr Abireku, calm yourself. That "scholar" is always like that; he abused me when I greeted him the other day.

MR OK You old fool, don't you know your daughter has committed bigamy by marrying another man under the native law? I want my wife, so I told Commission. She is going to be arrested.

MR TSI You lie!

MR OK You beast!

MR TSI (*Striking Mr Okadu on the lip with his forefinger*) Eye nten! You scorpion.

MR OK *Sacre c'chon!*

MR TSI Dam' swine!

They fight. Policeman tries to drag Mr Tsiba away. Old fisherman comes and parts them. Boys and women crowd round.

OLD FISH Yewura Tsiba, ma onka. W'ara nyim de nkyir'mba hon enyi nso hon mpenyinfu.

MR OK (*Turning angrily on old fisherman*) Shut up, you old savage stupid, or I will make this policeman arrest you.

OLD FISH (*To Mr Okadu*) Bo m' e, bo m'! Wu muwa a ehu nyi 'i a? W'enyibue nyi 'i a? Ehye atar 'ntsir n' na innyim nhon a hon mba bowu w' ba a?

POLICE (*To Mr Okadu*) Massa, make quick make we go gona house. Supitanna no get time.

IST Y W Egya Abireku, ma onka. Aburoba n' mbre otsi ara nyi n': oye nkutumpo. Edanu mi ma n' akyi a, ohye m'ahurba.

Mr Okadu and policeman burst through door, followed by Mr Tsiba and 2nd young woman.

IST Y W Aban asem wonka!

OLD FISH (*Going to his stool, and gathering his materials*) Iwiadzi ye yew! Iwiadzi ye yew!

Re-enter Mr Okadu through door L. followed by policeman dragging

NANA KAT You murderers! You accursed people! What has my grandchild done to you?

OLD FISH (...) Wait! What do they say Miss Araba has done?

2ND Y W They say because she has married another man, she is to be put in prison. They say that if those who are taken to be married in churches marry again before they are legally separated from their husbands, they break a law of the Government.

1ST Y W (...) Is Araba the first to offend in that way? Come, let us see what they are doing.

OLD FISH Wonders never cease! What has marriage to do with the Government?

Miss Tsiba. And pushing Nana Katawirwa and some other women. 2nd young woman tries to intercept policeman's hand. They rush, noisily, and exeunt R.

NANA KAT Ewudzifu! Ebusuafu! Mi ba aye hon den? *(Rushes R, and exit)*.

OLD FISH *(To 2nd Y. W.)* Twen! Wosi Ewuraba Araba aye den?

2ND Y W Wode oawar bio, 'ntsir n'wodzi n' rukotu fiadzi. Wosi wodzi wod hon ko Tsapir, na se wompe hon awar n' a, ibi su tu hon tsir nsa, na wonyi n' tsina a, nna oatu Aban mbra.

1ST Y W Huo: Araba nku na oaye dem? Bra ma yenkohwe. *(Exeunt, R. 1st and 2nd young woman)*.

OLD FISH Oboe! Awar su fa Aban hu?

MR ONY How hot it is (…) See? That Krooboy has shut the glass window (…) There goes the parson. I wonder where he is going at this early hour.

MR ONY Come in, parson!

[ACT FOUR]

SCENE ONE

Mr Onyimdzi's Office. Door, R. Window, C.

Mr Onyimdzi, *Seated at a desk working.*

MR ONY Oye hyiw ai! *(Looks round)* Hwe: krunyi n'atu ahwih-wetokura n' m'. *(Gets up and opens window. Looks out)* Sofu nyi n'. Anapa 'i dzi oruko hin? *(A knock is heard)* Come in!

Enter Half-crown.

MR ONY Well, Half-crown?

HALF God-juju-man come, sah.

MR ONY What are you talking about? What is "God-juju-man"?

HALF 'E be dem man way 'e get small collar for 'e neck, sah *(Indicating by a sign what he means)*.

MR ONY I see what you mean. So "God-juju-man" is "Minister" in your quaint lingo? Tell him say "Come". *(Exit Half-crown. A knock is heard)* Sofu bra!

Enter parson.

PARSON *(Shaking hands)* Morning, Lawyer! Peace be un—— *(Thinking it better not to bless Mr Onyimdzi)*.

MR'ONY Good morning, Mr Oyemfew! Please sit. What can I do for you?

PARSON I have come to see you about Mrs Okadu's case.

MR ONY You mean Miss Tsiba, I suppose?

PARSON Ah, Lawyer, no! no! no! I married the couple myself

[117]

in the house of God. "What God hath joined together let no man part asunder".

MR ONY I suppose there is no persuading you that you are quoting a text out of its context?

PARSON *(Placing his hat and umbrella on floor)* Well, I—

MR ONY Please, allow me. *(Takes up hat and umbrella and stands them in a corner).*

PARSON Well, I have come to warn you of the Vengeance that will descend on you for what you have done.

MR ONY What am I supposed to have done, now?

PARSON Vengeance is mine: I will repay, saith the Lord". You have assisted a heathen woman, Nana Katawirwa, to triumph over the Church in court.

MR ONY Is that all?

PARSON By winning the case of Rex v. Okadu, that Bigamy Case, you have enabled a pagan to triumph over the Church in public. "At the sound of trump, Satan's host doth flee". It is no use kicking against the pricks.

MR ONY Otherwise Saul would not have become Paul, eh, Sofu? It strikes me there is too much Saul and too little Paul in your composition.

PARSON I don't understand you. But I am glad you mention Paul. It shows that you know your Bible. Therefore you have committed a deliberate act of evil, and not a sin of omission. You have made the marriage ceremony in the Church ridiculous. You have made a holy sacrament a by-word in the mouths of the ungodly. For this, God will surely place your life in jeopardy. "In the midst of life, we are in death".

Re-enter Half-crown with a visiting-card.

MR ONY Well, Half-crown, why you no knock?

HALF I knock plenty: you no hear. So I come gi' you dem book.

(Handing card).

MR ONY *(Looking at card)* Tell 'em say "Come". *(To parson)* Don't go: but excuse me one moment, while I hear what Mrs Brofusem has come to say. *(Gets up and opens door).*

Enter Mrs Brofusem, lorgnette in play.

MRS BROF Good morning, Lawyer! I——Oh' Reverend, good morning!

MR ONY *(Shaking Mrs Brofusem's finger-tips)* Good morning, Mrs Brofusem! Warm, isn't it?

PARSON *(Shaking Mrs Brofusem's finger-tips)* Good morning, Mrs!

MRS BROF O, Mr Onyimdzi, please give me one of your photographs, and sign your name on it. You are famous now, because you have won the Bigamy case, which everybody has said you can't win. You know, in England all famous people sign their photographs, and give them to their admirers.

PARSON England must be very nice.

MR ONY But we are not in England now, you know, Mrs Brofusem.

MRS BROF It does'nt matter. We have gone to England: so we must do English things. English things are nice.

MR ONY But I havn't got a photograph handy. I—— *(A knock is heard)* Come in! Excuse me one moment, Mrs Brofusem.

Enter Half-crown.

HALF Plenty man come, sah. All get white cloth.

MR ONY White cloth? Oh! Nana Katawirwa's people. Where are they?

[119]

NANA KAT Sirs and Madam, we wish you a good morning!

MR ONY Thank you, grandmother!...

NANA KAT (...) I hope you have nothing more to do with my granddaughter. It was through you that this great trouble came upon her, though, by God's grace, it has passed... Sir, I thank you. If it had not been for you, my granddaughter would have been put in prison, Sir, I thank you.

MISS TSI Lawyer, I thank you.

MR ONY (...) Rise, grandmother, Mr Tsiba, Miss Tsiba, you, too rise. I also am to blame for the affair. Therefore I am glad that I was able to defend you. Do not thank me. I have said I will charge nothing.

NANA KAT (...) Sir, we thank you. We thank you. May God bless you.

ACT FOUR

HALF Three men live for clerk office. 'E lef' plenty man
outside.

MR ONY Tell dem three men say "Come". *(Exit Half-crown,
to Mrs Brofusem)* As I was saying, I havn't a photograph at
present. *(A knock is heard)* Come in!

*Enter Nana Katawirwa, Mr Tsiba and Miss Tsiba, in white,
with white clay masks on their faces.*

NANA KAT Yewuranum na Ewuraba, ye ma hon akyi o!

MR TSI Morning, sirs and ma'am!

MR ONY Y'ana! Good morning, Mr Tsiba!

MRS BROF *(Rushing gushingly at Miss Tsiba)* Hello, Erimintrude! I congratulate you! You win your case.

NANA KAT *(Intercepting Mrs Brofusem)* Muwo enyidadu de
enyi mi nana 'i nyi asem biara bio. Onam wu du na wenya
'funa pi a, Nyami n'adum ara, woabesin ko'. *(To Mr Onyimdzi
kneeling and bowing low)* Yewura, mida w' asi. Se m'enya
'wu a, nkye wodzi mi nana 'i atu fiadzi. *(Weeping softly)*
Yewura, mida w' asi.

MR TSI *(Kneeling)* I thank you with God, Lawyer Onyimdzi.
Araba, you too must thank Lawyer.

MISS TSI *(Kneeling)* Lawyer, mida w' asi.

MRS BROF Erimintrude, speak English. Oh, I forget.

MR ONY *(Raising Nana Katawirwa)* Nana, suer. Mr Tsiba,
Miss Tsiba, nhon su wonsuer. Mu su mika hu bi na asem n'
bee. 'Ntsir oye m' dew de m' aka hon asem ama hon ma
woedzi 'bim. Mma wonda m' asi. M'aka akyire hon de
minyingyi hon whii.

NANA KAT *(Bowing and weeping softly)* Ye-wura ye da w'asi. Ye
da w'asi pi. Nyami nhyira w'.

MR TSI No, sir, Lawyer Onyimdzi. Don't say you will not
charge. If you charge even a big amount, I will pay. Charge
something. I have many cocoa land, by the grace of God.

[121]

PARSON ...I will not meddle with the affairs of heathens.

NANA KAT (...) Is this the parson who gave evidence?

MR TSI Yes.

MR ONY Nana Katswirwa, do not take the parson's evidence to heart. He is a parson! he thinks everything he does is right. I don't think he went into the witness-box with an evil mind.

NANA KAT Did he not say that for his part he wished my grand-daughter would be convicted?

PARSON Yes. I did say so. Anyone who wants to get out of a marriage celebrated in a church should be put in prison. Anyone who thinks such marriages are void is a sinner.

NANA KAT Does your religion teach you to hate your neigh-bour's child?

PARSON Every Christian should detest heathens. Heathens are the enemies of God.

NANA KAT On the contrary, it is the heathen who is the child of God. Those who are satisfied with their customs they it is who are pleasing in the eyes of God. It was not from Europe that we learnt to know the nature of God. We worshipped God before white men came here.

MR ONY Let it pass.

MR ONY Mr Tsiba, you are kind. But I say I will charge nothing. It was through a silly joke of mine that Okadu came to imagine himself engaged to your daughter.

MR TSI *(To Mrs Brofusem and Parson)* Ma'am and Reverend, thank Mr Onyimdzi for us.

MRS BROF Did you not hear what your mother-in-law say just now? She say I am bad.

PARSON I will not have anything to do with this business. Minnyimfa m'anu ntu iwiadzifu hon asem m'.

NANA KAT *(To Mr Tsiba)* Sofu a ogyi dasi n' nyi 'i a?

MR TSI Nyew.

MR ONY Nana Katawirwa, mma ntsin Sofu 'i ni dasii n' du. Oye Sofu: odwin de dz'a obeye biara ye. Mundwin de odzi adwin bon gyi dasi.

NANA KAT Ye onu na osi oka n'anku a, nkye wodzi mi nana 'i tu fiadzi 'i bi a?

PARSON Nyew. Mara mi ke. Ibiara a orihwihwe atwi nehu efi asor-awar mu n'ose de wodzi n' tu fiadzi. Ibiara a odwin de asor-awar nye awar n'oye dzibonyenyi.

NANA KAT Wu Nyamisum mbre okyire w' nyi de fa wo nyanku ba hu tan a?

PARSON Krisiannyi biara wo de okyir abusumsorfu. Iwiadzifu ye Nyami n'atanfu.

NANA KAT Mbom, iwiadzifu na woye Nyami ni mba. Nhon a hon amambu so hon n' na woso Nyami su n' enyiwa. Ye Brofu bekyire hen nyank-upon nu suban: yesum Nyami ansana Abrofu riba ha.

MR ONY Woma onka.

PARSON No. I will not let this heathen speak like that to me. I must teach her that I am a minister of the gospel.

MR ONY Yes: in your own church: this is my office.

MR TSI Reverend, don't be angry.

PARSON I am a minister of the gospel. I have authority to speak before kings. You are only a lawyer *(To Mr Onyimdzi)* I am not afraid of you.

MRS BROF Reverend, you know, Lawyer Onyimdzi is famous: don't speak like that.

PARSON Mrs Brofusem, I don't know England; but I know my business. This lawyer has brought ridicule on the marriage ceremony in the church. I have come to tell him that God will abase him. "He hath put down the mighty from their seats." He will become like Nebuchadnezzar.

MR ONY Mr Oyemfew, once more I tell you that this is my office. If you will rant, rant from your pulpit to the fools who come to hear persons like you. You have already wasted a good deal of my time. Go away!

PARSON By the authority of the most high God, and of his son, Jesus Christ, I warn you that the vials of godly wrath will be poured on your devoted head for winning the Bigamy case, and helping to make of no avail the holy sacrament of Matrimony. "And I heard a great voice out of the Temple saying to the seven angels, Go your way, and pour out the vials of wrath upon the earth".

MR ONY You amuse me with your misquotations of the Bible. Please go. *(Rising)* Go and think of the evil your godly churches have done in breaking up and destroying the foundations of our simple morality. *(Opens door and holds it open)*.

PARSON You are a lawyer: a child of Satan. You do know not what you do. I have authority to curse you by wiping off the dust of your office from the soles of my feet. But, remember Nebuchadnezzar! "Pride goeth before a fall". *(Takes up his hat and umbrella)*.

MR ONY The fall of such parsons as you, no doubt. The pride of some of you parsons is incredible. Pass out!

NANA KAT Sir, the day is passing; you have much work to do. Therefore we will ask leave to go. We thank you very much.

MISS TSI Lawyer, I thank you very much.
MR ONY Don't mention it.

PARSON *(Turning in doorway)* I go. But remember that, through the laying on of hands, I participate in the holy Ghost which descended on the twelve apostles. Therefore my influence over my flock is great. I will see that not one of them brings you a case. I wipe the dust of your office from the soles my feet. Remember Nebuchadnezzar! *(Exit)*.

MR ONY *(Coming back to his seat)* Now, Mrs Brofusem, I shall send you a photograph as soon as I sit for one.

MRS BROF Thank you so much. I will come for it myself. Goodbye. *(Shakes hands with Mr Onyimdzi, bows to the rest, and exit)*.

Nana Katawirwa, Mr Tsiba, and Miss Tsiba get up.

NANA KAT Yewura, adzi rikyi; w'adwuma dosu. 'Ntsir yeba sira w' kwan na yeako. Yeda w' asi pi. *(Shakes hands with Mr Onyimdzi)*.

MR TSI Lawyer Onyimdzi, many thanks. *(Shakes hands)*.

MISS TSI Lawyer, mida w' asi pi. *(Shakes hands)*.

MR ONY Mma wonda asi. *(Opens door. Exeunt Nana Katawirwa, Mr and Miss Tsiba)*. The cheek of some of these parsons is absolutely insufferable. *(Reseats himself)* I am glad I won that case. It will knock a good deal of nonsense out of our young men and young women, who have been taught by half-educated missionaries to despise the native form of marriage, and to hanker after this foreign form which they know as "Holy Matrimony" with all the show and fuss attached to it in these parts. *(Goes on with his work)*.

SCENE TWO

Mrs Brofusem's Drawing-room. Doors R & L.

Enter Mrs Brofusem, R, in European garb, throws lorgnette on a chair, takes a photograph from her bag, and stands it on the piano. Then she fans herself.

MRS BROF O dear! It is hot! Too hot! But I have got it. I am sure he can't able to resist my new green umbrella, my new ten-guinea hat, and my new patent boots with white top. So he has give me the photo himself, and has sign his name on it. I go get frame for it. *(Exit, L.)*

After a few minutes, enter Nyamikye, L, drunk, in straw hat, an old frock coat, white trousers, brown boots, smoking a cigar, and holding a small withered branch in his hand.

NYAM *(Reeling, and clutching cover of piano-top to steady himself, thereby bringing down all the ornaments on piano)* I wh'——Wha'ah marra? Ha! Ha! Shome warra fa' dow'. I whi' man toray. I go shee my brorra. He crerk. He gi' me croe'sh. He gi' me cigar I whi' man. Ha! Ha! *(Scatters the flowers from a vase, and tries unsteadily to force the branch in his hand into the vase)* You fool *(to vase)* I want you carry tree, you no go do, eh? Gerraway! *(Places branch in an album)* Leaf dry good for sun, not for book. *(Reels to a glass)* Eh? Who you? Gerraway! Dam' Swine! *(Fights with his image)* Wharruwant? Never min': you my brorra: no fight. *(Picks up lorgnette)* Ah! I proper whi' man, now! I get shpe'clesh. *(Holds up lorgnette with one hand, and knocks down cigar-ash with the other)* Ha! Ha! Massha and Misshish all one!

Enter, L, Mrs Brofusem.

[129]

NYAM (...) Master, I beg your pardon. I do not know what
possessed me. I remember that I went to visit my brother,
the clerk, and that he gave me something to drink.

MR BROF Nyamikye, go and wait in my office.

MRS BROF Nyamikye, what's this? What are you doing here?

NYAM *(Imitating Mrs Brofusem)* He! He! How d'ee du? Hello, duckie! Duckie!

MRS BROF Get out of this room one time.

NYAM *(Staggering towards Mrs Brofusem, who moves backwards round the room to escape him)* Duckie, I put ash for ground. Kish me. I kish you. I whi' man all shame massha. Kish me, darling.

Mrs Brofusem falls over a chair. Nyamikye grabs her blouse. Mrs Brofusem gives him a hearty smack in the face.

MRS BROF *(Struggling)* How-dare——you?

NYAM You shtrong. I too shtrong. I too shtrong. I shtrong passh you. I kish you all shame you kish massha. *(Places his arm round Mrs Brofusem's neck)*.

Enter Mr Brofusem, R. in European garb.

MR BROF Good heavens. What's this? *(Rushes at Nyamikye, and pushes him down)* Duckie, what's the matter?

MRS BROF Nyamikye——drunk——and——trying—— to—— kiss me.

MR BROF *(Turning fiercely on Nyamikye, who, sobered by his fall, is standing rubbing his eyes)* What:

NYAM *(Kneeling)* Nuwura, mipa w' kyew. M'ara minnyi m' dz'a oba mu du. Mikê de mukuro mu nua a odzi krakyi n' ni nkyen, na oma m'nsa ma munumi.

MRS BROF I can't able to lift up my head again.

MR BROF Nyamikye, kotwen m' wo m'*office*. *(Exit Nyamikye)* Compose yourself, duckie. He did'nt know what he was doing. I have always known him to be a most well-behaved servant. I shall punish him severely for this lapse, all the same.

MRS BROF *(Flaring up)* Don't call me "duckie", you and your

MR BROF I am learning how to wear the native dress. The wearing of European clothes makes one too uncomfortable. Onyimdzi's success in Okadu's daughter's case together with the trouble into which Nyamikye got, here, the other day, have led my wife to wear native dress in the house. She says she will go out in native dress later. Nyamikye has shown me how to wear the cloth in a way that will keep it on my shoulder. Look! (...) You gather it up this way, then you throw it on you thus. Don't I do it well? Shoes have twisted my toes out of shape. Now that nothing squeezes them and the breezes fan them, is it bad? It has never struck me that sandals can be so graceful. Look at all these swellings on my foot: that is the result of imitating Europeans. In these days,

drunk servants—bringing them into the house to abuse me.
(Exit, L, in a rage).

MR BROF Well, I'm hanged. Behold the "white lady" hoist
with her own petard and blaming me for it! She must have
had a bad time of it. The whole room is in a state of confusion.
Poor woman! She was not so bad before she went to England.
It must have come as a great shock to her. *(Picks up a photograph from the floor)* Hello, Onyimdzi! And signed, too! I can
imagine my wife worrying him for it. I say, I almost forgot
about this startling affair. I must go and adjust matters.

SCENE THREE
The Same.

Enter Mr Brofusem, L, in native dress.

MR BROF Murusuasua etam fura. Atarhye ye atsitsi duduw.
Onyimdzi ni bim a odzi n' wo Tsiba ni ba n' n' asem n' mu
n', onyi Nyamikye n'amandze a edanu onya n'edan m' ha n',
woama nkyi mi yir ndaansa 'i owo fie a, ofura 'tam. Osi oye
kakra a, odzi bopue. Nyamikye akyire m'mbre mirsi fura
mi 'tam a, onkepa. Wonhwe o! *(Goes through the act of putting
on the cloth)* Efifa n' dem; na itu bo wu du dei. Nkyi m'ehu
fura? *(Sits and looks at his toes)* Asupatsir ama m'anansuaba
nyinara akyiekyia. Asu hwii mmia hon, na mframa su fa hu
'i omo a? Minnyim de mpabua ye few dem. Hwe apo-
wapow a woasusuw m'anan hu: Brofudzi ni nsunsuendu nyi
n'. Nde hen mu binum dwin de se woansua *helmet* a, onu
wonkotum ewia m' nantsiw. Naasu nkaanu wo dida mba-

there are some who think that they cannot walk in the sun without helmets, and yet, in former times, babies were laid out in the sun, and covered with baskets. I heard a new song the other day. It goes this way. (...):

"To whom is this unpleasant? I have bought cloth with my own money, and *you*, whom it does not concern, are green with envy."

Am I wrong? Is it not true that some of you are feeling too warm in the clothes you are wearing? I should'nt be surprised if somebody's boots were giving him a bad time of it: he, no doubt, wishes he were in sandals.

"To whom is this unpleasant? *I* have bought cloth
"To whom is this unpleasant? I am in sandals. I am in the native dress. If you like it, why, buy some."

I think there is someone calling me. I shall be back presently.

fraba wo ewia m', na wodzi kantan bua-bua hon du. Edanu
mitsi ndwim fufur bi a oaba ma worutu. Wontsie! *(Goes to
piano, and sings to his own accompaniment)*.

Wana na ompe adzi o?
Wana na ompe adzi o?
Midzi mi sika akoto 'tam,
Wusu ku ekyir w'enyi abir!

E? Mituei a? Nkyi atar a wohye 'i oama ehyiw dzi hon?
Ibir 'i ibi n'asupatsir rikan dwii, ni ya m' a nkye ohye
mpabua.

Wana na ompe adzi o?
Wana na ompe adzi o?
Mihye mpabua, mufura 'tam,
Wusu, se epe a, koto bi!

Oye m' de dz'a ibi rifre m'. Miriba. *(Exit, R.)*

Enter Mrs Brofusem, L, in native dress, with a photoframe.

MRS BROF Where is that photo? Ah here it is. *(Places photo in
frame)* How sweet of him to sign his name on it. I wanted to
hug him. I am sure Mrs Gush of Sea—O, I forget that it is
all finished. I am ashamed every time I see Nyamikye, that
horrid servant, although it is a week since it has happen. I
have made a big fool of myself. But I don't look a fool, I hope.
I wonder why I feel so comfy? *(Goes to a glass)* Why I have
forget that I wear native dress. It suits me, isn't it? Oh! What
nice long toes I get! They look sweet in sandals. D'you know,
I don't mind if my husband does not call me "duckie", now.
I have remember that Mrs Gush was fat, and she walk like
a duck. I have made up my mind to give up kissing. But my

[135]

MR BROF (...) Nyamikye, bring a clothes-brush.

2ND MAN (...) Oh! Oh!

1ST MAN Oh!
MR BROF That will do! Bring some whiskey and cigars.

husband is not sorry. Well, men are sometimes difficult to understand, not so? O, I am sorry. I will remember, in future, to speak Fanti to Fantis. Goodbye! *(Exit L.)*

Re-enter, R, Mr Brofusem, followed by two men in European clothes, rubbing their elbows and knees, and brushing dust from clothes.

MR BROF Please, sit down somewhere. *(Goes to door L)* Nyamikye, fa brosuu a wodzi prapra atar hu bra.

1ST MAN *(To 2nd man)* I get wound for my elbow.

2ND MAN *(Limping into a seat)* M'egya! M'egya. I knock my corn on a stone, and my head on the telegraph-post. *You* fall down. I only knock the telegraph-post.

MR BROF But did you not hear the lorry coming?

1ST MAN No, I hear a wonderful noise, and I think it is cow. I do not know that lorry make noise like cow.

2ND MAN Then we hear lorry noise, and people say, "Look out". Then we jump, and I knock the telegraph post, and he fall down.

Enter Nyamikye, L, with brush, and begins vigorously on 1st man.

1ST MAN M'egya! Don't rub hard. O!

MR BROF Oaye yie. Kefa *whiskey* onyi sigyar bra. *(Exit Nyamikye, L.)*

1ST MAN Mr Brofusem, *you* wear cloth?

2ND MAN Just what I was almost said.

MR BROF Yes. Why should'nt I wear cloth?

1ST MAN No. You have educated in England: you disgrace yourself if you wear cloth. O, I see: *(Goes to piano, and takes up a photo)* This is Lawyer Onyimdzi.

2ND MAN Let me see.

1ST MAN *(To Mr Brofusem)* You are following Lawyer Onyimdzi, now?

2ND MAN Yes. Just what I almost said.

[137]

Re-enter Nyamikye, L, with a tray on which are set a flask of whiskey, a bottle of soda, three glasses, and a box of cigars. Places tray on table and exit, L.)

MR BROF Now, gentlemen, help yourselves. You say I am following Onyimdzi? Of course, I am: he has more brains than I.

1ST MAN But you say long time that he is a fool because he wears cloth.

2ND MAN Yes. You say it to me too.

MR BROF *I* was the fool, at that time.

1ST MAN Funny. You wear sandals, too.

2ND MAN Yes. Sandals, too.

MR BROF Why not? My poor toes were tortured under the old regime of boots. They are happier now in sandals, under the rule of common-sense.

1ST MAN But you are not going out in cloth?

2ND MAN Not outside?

MR BROF I don't see any reason why I should'nt. I even wish I could go barefoot: but the soles of my feet are so confound-edly tender, now. The bushman, as we call him, is a better man than I in that respect.

1ST MAN Strange!

2ND MAN Strange!

1ST MAN But I hope you don't like the case Lawyer Onyimdzi win the other day. It means that all our wives married in Chapel are not lawfully married.

2ND MAN Yes.

MR BROF Hello! I never thought of that. I shall consult Onyimdzi on the point. Ah! But it is'nt so. I got engaged to my wife in the manner prescribed by our custom.

1ST MAN And I too.

2ND MAN And I too.

MR BROF So, you see, everything is all right. Onyimdzi's plea, in defending Miss Tsiba was that the Marriage Ordinance of 1884 had nothing to do with her.

1ST MAN That is what I can't able to understand.

2ND MAN I too.

MR BROF The reason is just this: that the Ordinance applies to those already married under the native law, who, later, desire to become full members of some church or other. So, all of us who married in churches are really married under the native law.

1ST MAN But you cannot marry more than one wife when you go to Chapel.

2ND MAN Yes, you cannot. *(Looks round the room)*.

MR BROF The native law, in its own way, recognizes only one wife, that is, the first wife. Any other wives that may be afterwards married are minor wives, subordinate to the first wife. If they belong to respectable families, not one of such minor wives will be given in marriage to the man who wants a wife or more besides his first wife, unless that first wife herself goes with the man's women-folk to ask for her.

1ST MAN That I never know.

2ND MAN And I too *(Continues to look round the room)*.

MR BROF That used to be the rule, when the native State was absolute in its power to deal with the members thereof, according to their deserts, and before undigested and indigestible foreign ideas began to eat into the vitals of the native social system. In the old days, when sons succeeded to ancestral Stools, the sons of the first wife had precedence, irrespective of age.

1ST MAN Is that so? *(To 2nd man)*.

2ND MAN Hmm? *(Gets up and looks under all the chairs)*.

1ST MAN *(To 2nd man)* What are you doing?

2ND MAN (...) If you will excuse my saying so (...)

MR BROF Bring two wooden spittoons. (...)

2ND MAN I am want spittoon, *Sebio*, if you smoke, you must use spittoon.

MR BROF *(Going to door, L)* I am sorry. I forgot to tell Nyamikye to bring you one. Nyamikye!

2nd man rushes out, R, with tightly closed lips.

1ST MAN *(Also rushing out R.)* I come.

Re-enter Nyamikye, L.

MR BROF Ko kofa adaka a anhwia wo m' n' ebien bra. *(Exit Nyamikye, L.)* There you are: they go and smoke when they should not smoke. The man who cannot smoke without wanting to use a spittoon has no right to smoke.

Re-enter R, 1st and 2nd man, wiping their mouths.

2ND MAN We want a "Ham Club". I don't want to talk of marriage. *(Sits)*.

MR BROF "Ham Club"? No thanks. Once I should have jumped at it. I am a good deal more rational, now. Fatty meats are not good for us out here, you know.

1ST MAN So you are Lawyer Onyimdzi's disciple, now?

2ND MAN You imitate him?

MR BROF No, I do not imitate him: we both view things from the same standpoint, now, I admit he put me into the way of reaching that stand-point.

1ST MAN All right. Let us finish to speak of the case. Anguanam can speak of his "Ham Club" afterwards.

MR BROF Yes. Onyimdzi proved that the girl was not engaged to Okadu at all, because there were no witnesses of the engagement.

1ST MAN But they went to Chapel.

2ND MAN Yes. Chapel.

[141]

1ST MAN Look here, Anguanam (...)

MR BROF That made no difference. You see, the proper witnesses to an engagement, under the native law, are certain relatives of both parties, and not the parties themselves. No such relatives could come forth as witnesses of the engagement that was said to have taken place at the garden-party at Victoria Park, some months ago.

1ST MAN But the parson joined their hands, and they signed their name in the book in the vestry.

2ND MAN Yes. I saw them go to the vestry.

MR BROF You are not following. I say that Onyimdzi proved that the marriage Ordinance of 1884 was for those already married under the native law, who, later, conceived the idea of becoming full members of a church. Miss Tsiba was not engaged to Okadu according to custom: she could not, therefore be married to Okadu under the native law.

2ND MAN But my friend say they went to Chapel. I saw them there myself. Now, let us talk of "Ham Club". Then we can get also fresh meat from the steamer, and ice, and fresh milk, and apples.

1ST MAN *Nhwe*, Anguanam, shut your mouth! Let us finish this talk first. So, Mr Brofusem, Miss Tsiba was not engaged?

MR BROF No. Onyimdzi showed that, under the native law, an engagement was really a marriage, the only difference being that the bride had not commenced to live with her husband. Pipes, tobacco and some money had to be sent to relatives and very intimate friends by the bride's people, after the bridegroom had sent clothing etc. to the bride, before the latter could be conducted, with torches, to the former's house, at night, on a day appointed by himself for the reception of his bride. The bride simply had no business to be in her husband's house, till after the first night, when everybody who was anybody knew that the bride had been *taken* to her husband's house, and had not gone there by

[143]

herself. You can see how strict the old people were, when you consider this taking of the bride to the bridegroom at night, and not before, on the day appointed.

2ND MAN *(Yawning)* Aw—w? Let's talk of fresh meat. *(Enter Nyamikye L, with two spittoons, which he places by 1st and 2nd man. Exit Nyamikye, L)* Ah! Now I can smoke. *(Re-lights his cigar)* The girl's child was born dead, not so.

1ST MAN Yes, and Okadu had to pay *ayifer**

2ND MAN Why, he engaged the girl, not so?

MR BROF If he had got engaged to her in the proper way, he would not have had to pay *ayifer*, because, in that case, he would have wronged himself. You see, under the native law, the man to whom a girl is engaged has the right to claim and receive *ayifer*, if anybody tampers with the girl. If he himself is the culprit, he has to claim *ayifer* from himself; which is absurd. But then he forfeits the right to send the girl away, the morning after the first night—the right of the man who finds that his bride is not virtuous. On the other hand, the bride, cannot be accorded the honours of the virtuous bride, nor does she pass through the real wedding ceremony, which, in the old days, took place eight days after the first night. We of these so-called enlightened days know little or nothing of these grand old customs.

2ND MAN *(Yawning)* Ah——h! When are we going to talk of the "Ham Club" *(Coughing sharply)* Oh! Ahem! Ahem!——

MR BROF Hello, what's up?

1ST MAN What's matter?

2ND MAN I——ahem——ah, ——h! I forget——myself. Ahem! Ahem! Ahem! Ahem! I——try to——swallow the smoke—— ahem! and make——make it——come out of——my ahem—— nose, like cigarette.

---

* The fine imposed by customary law on a seducer.

2ND MAN (...) Ah-h... It's killing me (...)

1ST MAN Let me slap your back.

2ND MAN *(Moving towards door. R)* No, Your hand too big.

MR BROF You will soon be all right. Don't cough so sharply.

2ND MAN I——ahem——can't. Ah——h, *muruwu (Falls over a chair. Mr Brofusem and 1st man go to his aid)* All——right, now. Ah——h! Ah——h!

1ST MAN What you say? You say my hand too big?

2ND MAN Yes. You come from bush, and go to school here. You get bushman's hand.

1ST MAN You drunk.

2ND MAN You drink more whiskey than me. *(To Mr Brofusem)* What about "Ham Club" Also the fresh meat, fresh milk, ice and apples?

MR BROF I don't want them. The meat, as a matter of fact, cannot be fresher than that sold here in town. If decent cattle were killed instead of bony ones, the meat here would be better than any you could buy from the boats.

2ND MAN Ah! But that is native meat. Fresh meat from the steamer is European meat. It must be nicer.

1ST MAN He talks like fisherman. I tell him about eating on steamer and he wants some. He never eat on steamer before.

2ND MAN *(To 1st man)* You drunk.

1ST MAN You too.

MR BROF Now, now, gentlemen, please shake hands, and forget all about it. Let us talk of something else now.

1ST MAN No. I am going I will not talk of this fisherman. He smells of fish. *(Exit R)*.

2ND MAN I, too, I will go. I will not stop here where that bushman has sit down. He smell of fish *(Exit. R)*.

MR BROF Well, I'm blest! Really, Onyimdzi was right all along the line. If only we were national, we should be more rational and infinitely more respectable. Our ways and our things suit our climate. For one thing, our drinks have

[147]

not the same maddening effect on our people as European drinks have. The people of the old days were wise indeed: if only we would follow the customs they left us a little more, and adopt the ways of other races a little less, we schould be at least as healthy as they were.